A TASTE OF HEAVEN

SHORT FICTIONS

R. SEBASTIAN BENNETT

This book is a work of fiction. Characters, events, and incidents are the products of the author's imagination. All names are invented, or are used fictitiously. Any resemblances to actual persons, living or dead, are purely coincidental.

Tailwinds Press
P.O. Box 2283, Radio City Station
New York, NY 10101-2283
www.tailwindspress.com

Published in the United States of America
ISBN: 979-8-9853124-2-3
1st ed. 2022

CONTENTS

A TASTE OF HEAVEN

Now comes the mystery!

— Henry Ward Beecher (last words)

MUSIC MINUS ONE

Don't worry.

At the edge of the driveway is Glover, the happy pooch with a clotted tail and yellowed teeth. He is bounding and loping, and then he is next to you, pressing his head against your thigh. He will pant and drool while you stroke him for hours, never too long. From the back of his throat comes a low friendly whine, the kind of whine that sounds harmonic, cadenced—even almost human—and stops while you rub under his neck or behind his soft flopping ears.

"Good Glover," you say, and pat the heaving chest and lumpy shoulder, allowing the dog to get hairs on you, a ribbon of golden fur down the inseam of your black jeans. Now Glover has wiggled between your legs, and he is pushing his nose into your crotch. Why do dogs always do that? It's so embarrassing, especially when you're at your boyfriend's house on a date and he only laughs. But you don't mind because you love Glover, with the bad breath and dislocated pelvic disks that make him drag his hind feet when he wakes up from a nap. Yes, you love your dog, even though you haven't seen him for five months. Glover remembers. He remembers your perfume perhaps. Of course he understands that you thought about him and missed him while you were away at college without any pets at all—except for the cricket that lived in the corner of the dorm room and only chirped during the day (you had an agreement), and it never spit or dripped out any brown juice, ever. Crickets do that, they say.

Glover has a tick. A gumdrop-sized fat gray tick with an embedded head deep under the skin of the poor old dog's front leg. You swallow and clench teeth as you pluck it—pop it—off the white "glove" of his foreleg, which is how he got his name. You have to wash your hands when you get inside, must remember. Now you just stroke Glover's head, the tips of your finger in the fur of his crown, around the bony bump in the middle. Is that the cerebral ridge? You gaze deep into the dog's round dull eyes. He has cataracts, poor thing. He looks back at you. Sometimes you can actually see trust; it comes as a gleam. Glover missed you. He loves you, and it's okay that his hind legs leave eczema skin flakes on your shoes.

"Hoh! Melinda's back!" The deep resonant voice of your father, Max, comes from one of the top windows of the huge Colorado timber house that seems very old because Max built it from used lumber that he got from demolition sites. You saw them once—abandoned schools and shipyards from the forties and fifties, cracked toilets and rusty pipes and mahogany flooring that looks even better than new when reinstalled, re-sanded, and stained so it glows. Max (it doesn't seem so strange to call your father "Max" now that you're a college girl) got it all so cheaply from that man with the infected nostrils, the edges red and scabby like he ought to be in a Victorian children's book as a warning to little kids who pick their noses. Now Max is at the front door in the same old suspenders and Birkenstock sandals. He still has long pony-tailed hair to his elbows, which makes him look like a beast, a bridge troll, if he lets it down—so you told him his profile is striking and he ought to keep his hair pulled back in a clasp or a braid. It was daughter-to-father closeness, fashion advice, intimacy that he will always cherish, and you will too.

When you hug him hello, you give a real hug with arms all the way around his sloping shoulders. You're glad he doesn't have that awful pipey smell anymore since he stopped smoking, and you know he doesn't mind that you're not wearing a bra and it's obvious in a T-shirt, but he never cared much for that uptight crap. Besides, *braless* is in style now. You cut the line at underarm hair, though. Max's belly is round—not flabby—a big hard belly pushing against your abdomen. It's true that he gained thirty pounds, you see as you lean against him and gaze at that face with the crooked nose and always-needs-a-shave roughness; the face that read you *Little House in the Big Woods* and *Lord of the Flies*—until Piggy got killed. That face didn't crease, didn't grimace when you put regular dishwashing liquid in the electric washer—two whole cups—and it foamed, spurted, surged out onto the maple hardwood kitchen floor before the sealer set, warping and ruining the tongue-and-groove nailing, so the workers had to come rip it up with big crowbars, mallets, and chisels. They stuck in adobe tile instead, which is rough and lumpy and beaded, but beautiful in its own way, right? Like an old mission floor . . .

Max has his arm around your shoulders, loosely, casually, like in that first picture of him and Mom—you always called her Mom, not *Leonara*. Maybe your shoulder feels like Mom's to him, does it? Eight years ago—does he remember? The hoarse raspy wheezing . . . That final terrible time—heat piercing the forehead, searing, falling through the floor—when the nurse wouldn't let you go into Mom's room anymore. She wouldn't let you open hospital door number 14. But you shoved and charged and turned the big round handle with the gold metal insert for the key; you twisted the cold metal knob and pushed hard to open the heavy door—Mom was gone! They'd taken her. But you could still smell the menthol rub she'd wipe on her chest, a big smear with two fingers into the blue jar and it came up like mucous, and Mom had to keep doing it, couldn't stop. She stroked it, spread it over her breasts even though Max said that camphor was a suppressant from a homeopathic point of view, and probably caused asthma and allergies in children because the irritant or whatever couldn't escape through the skin pores anymore. "Exude" is what he'd said.

With Max's meaty arm still around your shoulder, both of you turn to gaze at the big mountain behind the house. It looks like an elephant profile, with a long thick trunk and two front legs composed of jagged rocks, pine, and sagebrush—where once you heard that whimpering, screeching, miauling from behind the rock and Max went up to see. It was a baby mountain lion. A kitten the size of a cat that didn't even have claws or real big fangs yet. Just little paws with black skin pads and a wiggly stump of a tail. Its mother was gone. All gone. She probably got caught in a coyote trap or was shot with rock salt by some of the weirdos that lived in those shacks on the other side of the quarry. That's what the ranger said when you took the lion cub to the station, and they put it in the cage next to the hoot owl with a broken twisted foot.

Glover is wagging his tail, pounding it against the truck now. Maybe that's how he clumps it. He's so excited that you're home, he shivers and jumps and bangs his head on the bumper—he lets out a yelp.

"Awww, poor Fat Baby," says Max.

"Fat Baby?" you ask, and take a step forward. The

cheap polyester band around the top of your K-mart panties digs into the soft skin below your navel. Your jeans are too tight at the crotch because you probably put on about ten pounds at school. You can't steam vegetables or make brown rice with tahini sauce there, the way you would at home. "Who's *Fat Baby*?" you ask, and feel your chin thrust forward.

Max stops walking and turns his hairy chest with the gold chain that matches the bulbous carnelian ring with Persian etching that you only pretended to like. He still wears it on his pinky. "Oh—*Glover* . . . Fat Baby. That's what we call him now," says Max. "Just for fun. Kind of a cutie-pie name, you know? Doesn't really mean much. Celeste thinks he looks like a chubby baby who doesn't know he's drooling." Max only holds your gaze for a moment.

The big front door creaks open. You hear it swing on those oiled brass hinges and you feel the dark of the hall behind your back. You turn to see a tall, plump woman with freckles, and bright red hair. She's wearing a Guatemalan peasant skirt and a stained purple sweatshirt with the collar cut out. "Hey, Celeste! Come and meet Melinda!" Max grins and his cheeks puff up. You toss back your hair and shake Celeste's pudgy hand. She takes too much vitamin E and eats too many nuts, you can tell already from her oily palm. She also probably eats too many carrots and oranges because her skin has a funny yellow glow, which a person really can see if they're sensitive enough. Probably there's a citrus scent, too. Does Max smell it in bed with her?

"Hi," says Celeste in a nasal voice. She widens her eyes as if she's talking to a toddler that needs encouragement. Of course, Celeste is probably nervous to meet you. So you give her that nice smile of yours and try to be open and loving as you smile, feeling your dimples, and you don't really look her in the eye. Why can't she wash the egg off her sweatshirt or comb her hair better? Your hair won't ever be greasy and matted like that, and certainly not in five years when you're exactly as old as Celeste is now.

"I like your sweatshirt," you tell Celeste. "It's a pretty violet color." And Max grins wider, revealing uneven teeth. He looks like he might salivate over his bottom lip as he takes Celeste's hand and squeezes it. Then he kisses it.

You go into the house, into that big front hall with the white plaster lion's head nailed to a beam. They should really paint the head so it won't be so garish, so glaring. The same old, deep musty smell is in the house. It's a good homey wine-and-wheat aroma that greets you just like before. It surrounds you and enters your nostrils as you walk into that hall you knew so well, where your dates would step in and wait by the thigh-high clay satyr vase until you came out of your room near the top of the banister and walked down the wide stairwell like a princess, like Cinderella in her castle. Cinderella never needed to pad her brassiere, either.

At the end of the hall, bathed in the gray light from the window in the arch of the roof, the widow's peak, is an odd statue. It's about five tall, egg-shaped, with spheres of purples and blacks and reds in layered paint, thick with ridges like scars. Inside the circular casings are painted metallic rings, pearls, and baubles. Near the bottom, in one of the lower cells, lurks what seems to be a mouse head. "Oh, you haven't seen Celeste's sculpture yet, have you?" asks Max in a breathless grating voice, pausing to stare at the thing as if it is a gift from the heavens, a symbol of the universe, of eternity itself. "Celeste is really—I mean really—an artistic genius."

"Oh, stop . . . " Celeste coos, sighs, and snuggles against Max. You can hear it, see it, know it, even though your back is turned. Their foot shuffling gives it away. Finally, you turn around.

"My professor says this piece is *post-structurist,* via *deconstructurism,*" says Celeste. "But art is just . . . " She closes her eyes and leans back her head. "I mean . . . all art, is just life."

You don't look at Celeste. "Yeah, it's great," you say, above the rushing water from the toilet near the den, which never stops flushing, unless you remove the cover and reach deep inside through the tank water—clean water, Max said—and pull at the black rubber thing that leaves a skunky-smelling mark on your fingers for two days that won't wash off.

Max never put up your art in the house.

Not even the pictures from art camp. He said he couldn't drill or tape on the dry wall. Did he still have his birthday picture that you made him, "Platypus in Lilacs," on the floor in his office?

The back of your neck burns, prickles. You pace down the corridor and take a long deep breath under the sand-blasted wood ceiling beams, calm beams, peaceful warm wood. You wander into the kitchen, which has an ammonia detergent smell even though the floor is very dusty, and dirty macaroni-infested pans and chipped mugs lie strewn on the counter like war refuse. You sniff the cleaning fluid again. At least Celeste cleans sometimes. Or did the detergent just spill? They haven't taken out the trash, either. It's flowing from green plastic sacks and—that spice rack! The tri-level, K-Tel *Revolvo-Rack* turntable that you bought Mom for Christmas when you were in sixth grade and only had enough money to shop at Gemco.

The Revolvo is shoved into the trash bag, feet up, top over like a sinking hulk. It's coated with brown honey goo and clotted dead black ants.

Max thumps in and you hope he's alone and he is. "It's good to have you back," he says, and gives you another hug, very close to his chest, but you pull away at the last minute—can't help it—but cover yourself, automatically cloak the rebuff with a question, smooth as glass. "How's your music going?" you ask, and raise your eyebrows, ripple your lips as if his answer is everything you've been waiting for.

"Good, yeah."

"Great!" You caught him before he felt the tenseness in your shoulders, before he heard the missing conversational half-beat as you backed into the pantry cabinet with the canned yams from years ago. The corner shelves dig into your spine and swelling hips. You caught him in the uptake and he didn't feel it. Didn't flinch. In some ways, he could be dense as well as brilliant. Good.

"But it's the same old bullshit at the clubs. The same prissy cliques at the gigs." He shakes his head in tiny frissons, jello-shivers of the skin wattle under his chin, mostly from alcohol, probably. "Listen, Jesus, I haven't even shown you yet! They have these new tapes now, *Music Minus One*. The best jazz players in the world—and it's perfectly syncopated, perfectly set up. You know exactly how many measures to solo." His eyes get wider, bulge, as if he's just had an adrenaline shot. His cheeks flush, his fingers wiggle. "Hey, why don't I play a little for you now? A little concert. It's wonderful, really. I can just play as much as I want, practice right here for as long as I . . . Would you like that?"

You nod enthusiastically, deep neck nods, and smile

wide in total approval, utter enthusiasm that you know he needs, yearns, and follow his big frame down the hall, into the living room.

"Hey, Celeste!" he bellows—too shrill, too raucous. You pop your eardrums as his voice booms forth, resounds in the hall, echoes up the stairs to the little room that used to be Mom's study at the end of the corridor, and hear Celeste's squeaking, childish voice. "Ye-es?"

"Come on down. I'm giving a little concert."

"Oh, great!" Celeste chirps. She's learned the utter approval, total response, too . . . Wearing white fuzzy bunny slippers with one ear missing and one torn, she wriggles down the stairs and takes a seat in the big leather arm chair behind you, against the wall.

You stay standing, thighs stiff.

Max bends over the Fender amp and clicks the toggle switch so a burst of static, a huge throb pumps out of the speakers like a sword thrust. You shudder. Now Max is pulling out his saxophone, the big one with green tarnish around the Selmer insignia. "I'm playing tenor a lot now," he says. A metronome sounds, recorded, digital, precise as a time bomb counter; chirring clicks bite into the wood floors, bounce, shimmer off the horrid chandelier with hanging crystals like falling nails.

The intro has started, swishing snare and strumming bass. A muted trumpet riff. Max is nodding, intent, serious as if God's voice is emerging—or as if he is about to speak to God. He takes the mouthpiece to his lips, puffs out his cheeks. Your back begins to sway as the first deep low rounded notes pour forth, shoot out, float from the bell of the horn and hover in the air. Long, haunting minor tones. Then the melody starts. It is the theme from *Black Orpheus* that Mom and Max used to hum to you. They used to hum it together before you fell asleep . . .

You fight back the hot sting of tears, don't let them out, don't even show their need. Just open your eyes wider, so the moisture can't gather. You bend and rock, and nod the knowing nod of years in the clubs, the understanding timed nod of an experienced jazz listener. You roll your neck to the beat, and catch Max's deep green eyes as he gazes at you over the neck of the sax. The music pours forth under his fingers, fast and smooth despite their size. Tremolos of color, actually prismatic, seem to flow from the bell of the horn. Loud, yes but wafting, spewing reds, greens, and golds.

You smile—and don't turn around. You won't look at Celeste. This song is for you. It is *your* tune. And you swing your back some more, and hips too—the rounded bottom that all the men like—you've aimed it at Celeste. Accidentally, though . . . You're rolling it now, all to the beat of course, switching your weight from one leg to the other, pushing forward your breasts. Then you hear it—the grating slide of the arm chair, the metal feet scraping across that rich red lustrous wood floor. And you can see Celeste's tall profile and her clumped hair as she stands up, swivels, and leaves the room, pacing into the hall, plodding away in her ripped rabbit slippers.

Max doesn't see. He has turned to stare out the windows now, to face the mesa as he lifts his knees as if walking in place. He blows the searing, whirring, ascendant notes out the door. The panes tremble, the trees rustle, and you spread your legs just a bit wider, over the floor.

THAT GOLD DIAMOND LIGHT

PLEASE LEAVE A MESSAGE AFTER THE TONE:

Hi, Vivian . . . It's Murray. I need to ask you something. Did you mean it when you said I had a psychic connection with the cat?

When I was at your apartment last week, Miko kept staring at me, and you said he never did that to anyone before. His eyes were so wide open. I could see the gold color—cats have that gold diamond light in their eyes.

You didn't like my cat noises, but didn't I sound like a real cat? Everyone says I do. To meow, you have to tense your throat hard and make a tight little sound, because cats only have little throats. It hurts humans to meow. And honestly I don't think you showed enough appreciation for my cat noises. I mean, it wasn't very nice of you to say I was *immature*.

I sensed that you might be worried about Miko. Are you worried?

I have to tell you something. When I left your place last Friday, he followed me out to my car. I didn't call him or anything, he just followed me. When I opened the driver door, he jumped in. I said, "Miko, you're not supposed to be in the car." He just stared at me again. And then he lay down on the seat. So I took him home.

Maybe this sounds weird. But I knew it was right. He chose me. Miko wanted to be with me. It was his decision. So don't freak out and call the police. Even if you did call the cops, they wouldn't do anything because I didn't steal Miko. He wanted to come with me.

I don't think he misses you very much. Yesterday, when we were watching TV, Miko was licking my neck. We were watching that show about the guy who raises lions—the show you said was fake. It's not fake. The guy just has a special relationship with the lions. That's why he can lie down with them and they don't hurt him.

Maybe I should have called you before, because you might be worried about Miko—but I knew you had the software project to finish at work, and that's why I didn't bother you.

I'm a cat person. I don't think you're a cat person. But you're not a dog person either. I don't know what you are. Maybe you're a *computer* person . . .

Wait a minute, Miko just walked in. He smelled the sushi I ordered. Miko and I like sushi. You don't like sushi. You like tofu. Did you know that ninety percent of soy products are genetically engineered? Miko and I don't eat genetically engineered food.

I'm petting him right now. He's super-relaxed. He wants me to pet his cheek. When I touched your cheek on the couch, you tensed up. That wasn't very nice.

Okay—wait. I'm holding the phone near his head. "Miko, do you want to talk to Vivian?"

He doesn't want to talk to you. He's licking my arm. Cats' tongues are so bristly. But they're warm. Did Miko lick you a lot? Did he lick your neck?

Anyway . . . so call me I guess. I guess you can come over. If Miko wants to go back to you, you can take him back. We have to let Miko decide, right? I mean it's only fair, right?

Listen—can you hear it? Miko's purring very loudly while I'm petting him.

It's a heartbeat motor. I can feel it.

STREN

Tomato George drove us up toward the mesa in his vegetable truck. He knew of a pond out behind old Ferguson Ranch. I pressed a new box of lures between my knees and stared down at its shiny top. In my pocket, I had a new box of purple *Stren* line. The old pick-up truck creaked and went faster. A crate of carrots slid down the bed in back and clanked against the tailgate. George looked over at me. "Did you buy stink bait?"

"Nah," I said.

"Gotta have stink bait if you're goin' for catfish. They smell it and get interested. Then they suck it. When you see the line wiggle, you set the hook. Hard . . . " He spit out the window.

I glanced down at the reel of my fishing pole, wedged between my feet. "No, I wanna get bass," I said. "Big ones." I turned the handle on the reel. It made a good loud click.

George popped open a can of Coors with one hand

and held the steering wheel with the other. "Can't fish without beer. It's the law . . . " He smiled. "Want one?"

I hesitated. I was flattered by George's offer. He made me feel like just another one of his friends, even though I was only twelve. But I had worked hard all day, worked a man's day, unloading vegetables from the van. George was paying me three fifty an hour, so I made twenty-eight bucks, enough to buy a cheap rod, line, and a few lures. "Yeah, I could use a beer," I said, and reached for a can. It felt good and cold in my hand. Out loud, I read the metallic print: "Brewed with pure Rocky Mountain spring water."

"*Kerz*," said George.

"What?"

"Call it *Kerz*. Then you're cool."

"Kerz," I repeated. "Yeah, I drink Kerz!" We laughed, just as the pickup hit a big pothole, shuddered, bounced, and spilled beer on both of us.

"Right on!" said George. He turned onto a muddy road and drove up a hill. Then we almost drove into the pond. George said, "We're here," and slammed on the brakes.

It was a small pond, only about a hundred fifty feet across. Scrub oak and tall reeds surrounded the pond on three sides. On the open side stood a small dock with peeling gray paint. I pressed open the door handle and jumped out of the cab, grabbing my gear. George swung out and pulled a bottle of "Sir Edward's" Scotch from under the front seat. He showed me how to tie the line on my reel and thread it past the bail arm. "Time to fish!" I yelled.

"Quiet now," George said softly, "or you'll scare 'em."

"I know," I said. "I've fished a lot before."

"Oh," George smiled. He went to get a pole out of his toolbox.

We moved over to the dock. George had a plastic container of worms. He dug one out and it wiggled between his fingers. Then he wrapped it around his hook, wound it double and pierced it twice, so it made a twitching bundle. I didn't like worms; I didn't like the way they squirmed. I picked out a bright red lure instead and tied it to my line.

George cast out first, a long smooth cast that flew directly to the center of the pond and dropped in place. The water barely even rippled. "Nice one," I said. Holding the rod low behind my shoulder, I tried to imitate his cast. I swung the rod forward and stepped into the throw, just like George did. But my line got caught on a tree overhead. I squinted, peered up into the leaves, and saw the line tangled on a small branch. A bird hopped over, fluttered its wings, cocked its head, and pecked at the red lure. "Dammit," I said. It felt good to curse.

"Don't get upset now," George said in steady voice. "You'll probably have to go and cut the line. No point in messing around with that tree."

He was right. A quick slash with my penknife, and the problem was solved. I tied on another lure. This one was orange with gold fringe.

"There you go . . . " George opened the scotch and sipped at it from the bottle while I got ready to cast again. "Not so fast this time," he said. "Follow through with your whole arm."

But the cast landed in the brush on my left. Didn't even make it to the water. I jerked the pole hard. The lure was stuck tight. So I whipped out my pocketknife again.

"Wait a sec," said George. "How many lures do you have left?"

"One."

"Better go find it. Otherwise you'll soon be usin' worms . . . " He smiled. He knew I didn't like those worms.

I turned so he couldn't see me blush and headed toward the bushes. They crackled as I pressed in deeper. The reeds were thick. My arm got scratched and I heard some bees. Then I spotted the line snaking through a puddle, and there—the lure was caught between two rocks. I stepped forward and my shin bumped against something hard, something buried in the thicket. With both hands, I tugged at the weeds, pulled back dried grass and mud vines. It was a canoe!

"George! George! I found a canoe!" I yelled.

He didn't answer. He must have gone to the truck for

beer. Then I realized it was stupid to shout. Might have scared all the fish away. I worked hard, digging and kicking at reeds to expose the rest of the canoe. I dragged it out. It was a good canoe. A little battered maybe, but it looked like it would float. There was even a paddle. I couldn't wait to put the canoe in the water. This would be my boat, my bass boat. I'd use it to fish the bluff. That's where all the big fish hid. I dragged the canoe over to the dock.

George was still out by the truck. I could hear him singing. But I didn't call to him. I pushed the boat into the water and watched the way it floated. No leaks. I smiled, smoothed back my hair—the canoe started to drift away! I lunged for it, and missed. Luckily, I still held the paddle in my hand. So I thrust fast and secured the canoe until I could grab it again. Then, holding my rod in one hand, I climbed aboard.

The canoe swayed a lot, but I centered my weight in the middle to steady it. I took a few strokes and glided from shore. Just to get the feel of the canoe, I paddled it around a little. "She's made solid," I said under my breath. Then I thought about the way I called the boat a "she," like a captain would . . . I knew my father wouldn't want me out in a boat without a life preserver. He didn't even like fishing. But George and I had finished work early for the first time, and we were celebrating.

When I was ready to cast, I swung the lure toward the reeds. It plopped in just where I wanted. I let it sink a bit, then bobbed the tip of the fishing pole. This made it seem like the lure was swimming through the water. The fish would be attracted by the motion and go to bite. Suddenly, I got a huge hit—the line went taught and my pole bent almost double. Then the line went slack again. "He spat it out," I said quietly. But I kept bobbing the pole, concentrating. I set the drag just in case the fish was still there, waiting to take the lure and run with it. Then I felt him again, stronger this time. The reel screeched and vibrated as he took the lure and swam toward the deep water. I wound in some, and then I had him firm.

But this fish was smart. When he couldn't run any more, he headed back to the reeds where the line would tangle and break. I jerked the spindle round as fast as I could and reeled in more line. This was a big fish. He was actually towing me, boat and all, toward the reeds. "Oh, no you don't, fish . . . " I said, and held the pole tight. My fingers were numb.

I heard George shouting and, out of the corner of my eye, saw him jumping up and down on the dock. But I had to concentrate. I tightened the drag all the way and wound in line. I was gaining on him. Then I saw the fish for the first time, close to the surface, swimming like hell. He was big all right, about two feet. The sun gleamed on his back as he surged through the water. He had tan and gold marks on his sides, and silver fins. I took a deep breath. He was beautiful. There was still time—I felt the bulge of the pocketknife in my back pocket. I could cut the line and set him free . . . No. I was a fisherman. A fisherman always keeps his catch. I jerked the rod up in a quick yank, and then reeled faster.

"Go for it!" George yelled. He was pulling at his hair. Now there were only a few feet of line between me and the fish. I could tell he was a bass, a great big bass. With two hands on the rod, I tried to lift him out of the water. The pole bent in half, almost in a circle, so I grabbed the wet line and lifted out the fish. The line dug into my palms, but didn't break. *Stren* was supposed to be extra strong. That's what George had said. The hook and lure were deep inside the fish. I couldn't even see them. I only saw the bright arching of the bass as he emerged from the water and fought me from the air.

I set the fish in the bottom of the boat and held him down with both feet. His stomach was fat. In the middle of it, there was a weird, round golf-ball size bulge. His fins flapped like little wings and bubbles came out of his gills. He flopped around for a while, then lay still.

As I paddled to shore, George was whooping and cheering on the dock. His eyes were red from drinking. He ran to get a bucket, then helped steady the canoe and reached for my fish. "Well, damn, that's the biggest bass I've ever seen! Must weigh twenty pounds. You got the granddaddy of 'em all!" He beamed at me, took out a pair of needle-nosed pliers from his pocket and stuck it down the fish's throat. He tugged at the hook, then worked it side to side. I winced. The bass shuddered and gagged. Blood dripped down George's hand.

"What's that round thing on his stomach?"

George pressed it with his thumb. "Feels kinda hard. Maybe he ate a lure . . . Or maybe he ate a turtle. Big fish like this gets mighty hungry."

I looked down at the canoe and the oblong, damp spot in the bottom where the fish had lain. George got a bucket and went down to the pond to fill it with water for the fish. "You better put that canoe back where you found it," he said.

On the way home, I couldn't stop thinking about the fish. George had put him in the back so he wouldn't smell up the truck, but I could see him through the rear window. I could see his eyes. George had said the bass was a *granddaddy.* He had probably spawned a lot of babies and probably got hooked a lot, but escaped. And survived. That's how he knew to head for the reeds. But I had caught him, and taken him with skill. I stole another glance through the window. Next to George's boxes of tomatoes—the overripe ones that we couldn't sell in the parking lot at Tastee Freeze—the bass seemed greener than before. He was almost vertical in the bucket. His head stuck out a bit. His mouth kept opening and closing.

George couldn't stop talking about the fish. "Yeah, he's

a biggie all right. He'll be good eatin' no doubt. And you landed him like a pro. Let's stop at the store and show him off to all the folks."

It took a second for this to sink in. George wanted to go exhibit the fish. To measure him and stick his finger in its bloody throat. But I didn't want to parade him around. I didn't want anyone to see him.

"No," I said.

"No, what?"

"Let's not take him to the store."

George looked puzzled for a moment. Then he said, "Oh, I get it. You want to go show him to your old man right away. Okee dokee."

We pulled into my driveway. George ran out to look at the fish again. I wiped some slime from my hand onto my pants. I was glad that my father wasn't home.

"He's still alive! Still alive!" George announced. He was giggling. "You'll have to hit him with something so he dies. Do you got any beer?"

"Can you take care of him for me, George?" I asked. My stomach hurt.

George looked at me for a moment and laughed. "Sure, buddy. Go get me a rock."

My legs were stiff, aching. I forced them to move, consciously lifted each thigh, swung forth each foot and set it back down. Obediently, I went to look for a rock. I found one near the dumpster and gave it to George. Then I closed my eyes. With three heavy thuds, he hammered the fish.

"He won't die. He's tough," George reported. "Go get me some tin foil."

He wrapped up the bloody bludgeoned bass, then handed him to me. I didn't want to hold him. I didn't want to touch the fish anymore, but I couldn't refuse now. I took him in two arms. He was very heavy. I felt him move inside the foil.

"Go put him in the freezer," said George.

My hands burned. I carried the fish to the storage freezer in the garage. I opened the door and gently lay him on the bottom shelf. Then I closed the door.

The rattling sound of my father's Volkswagen diesel sounded in the driveway. I watched George walk over to the car and begin talking excitedly, even before my father got out. George grinned and spread his hands wide, demonstrating the length of the bass. Then he made a fist and beat it against his palm. Through the open car window, I could see my father nodding slowly, but he didn't look anywhere near as excited as George.

I walked outside to the car. My father stepped out. He leaned against the fender and adjusted his glasses on the bridge of his nose. His expression was curiously blank. "Heard you caught a big bass," he said.

"Yeah."

"You should have told me you were going up to the mesa . . . " He stared at me. "We can't eat that bass."

"What?" I said.

George looked shocked. "Why not?"

"They used to farm a lot up there. Back before the EPA. Those ponds are full of DDT and mercury. You can't eat those fish. They're sick. They could cause cancer."

A wave of nausea gripped my body. I swallowed, blinked and managed to stay calm. I wiped my hands on my pants again. "What should we do with it?"

My father didn't answer. His jaw tensed.

"Throw it in the garden," said George. "The birds'll eat him. They'll be happy."

"No. It could poison the birds, too," said my father. "You should have told me you were going up there."

I felt numb. A hot flash ran up my neck. "So what can we do? He can't swim anymore."

"Is he still in the freezer?" my father asked.

I nodded.

"Wait until he's dead. The freezer will put him to sleep . . . " He closed his eyes. He was silent for a long while.

"Then what?" I asked.

"Build a fire back where we burn brush. Wait till the flames are least three feet, and put the fish in the fire. Stay and watch till all the flesh and scales are burned off, and make sure no animals get any of it."

I stared at the ground.

"Wait until only bones are left." My father's eyes narrowed. He took off his glasses, then wiped his brow. "And one more thing . . . "

"What?"

"Tell the fish you're sorry."

INCARNADINE

I like to dress up as a priest. I wear black shoes and black pants with sharp creases. "Extra starch, even on the slacks," I tell the dry-cleaning girl. Of course I have a black coat—coal gray, actually, single-breasted with European slits in the back. My shirt is really the most important article, with a virgin white strip under the throat. But the shirt is not an authentic priest's shirt. It's a black *Rip Curl* surfer's T-shirt which the designer chose to emblazon with a white collar, as a matter of surf fashion I suppose. Thus I am not dressed entirely *de rigueur.*

Since my shirt is not authentic, and it is of the surf variety instead of the clerical, I'm not certain that I look like a real priest. I know there is an ambiguity in my appearance. I am either ministerial or bohemian, blessed or outcast. It is up to the masses to decide. If they want me to be a priest, I shall be one. If they need me, I am there . . .

Last Saturday, late on a warm afternoon in La Jolla cove, it was a perfect time to sit in my favorite café, Babiole, which has an array of imported coffees and teas. They keep a bowl of glass eyes—tigers and lapis and blue quartz—behind the counter. The first customer every day gets to choose which ones to slip into the optical sockets of a wooden chimpanzee head near the door. The eyes light up electronically. I've never been the one to do this. Once I saw a woman do it, though. I watched her bend over, pick out a glistening white oculus, and sink it in. That was a very long time ago.

I was sitting in my favorite booth near the back of the café, a perfect spot which enabled me to observe all the other patrons and keep watch. I ordered my favorite coffee, Indonesian Blend, that's quite potent if it's brewed right. But if Indonesian isn't brewed correctly, it will give you bad dreams. On the table lay a newspaper, the local *Free Press*, with personal ads in the back. "Women Seeking Women," my favorite section, unfortunately had no ads in it (perhaps all the lesbians were satisfied). So I looked for my second choice, "Women Seeking Men." I took a sip of my coffee. Then a husky female voice came from behind me. "What are you reading, Father? The Scriptures?"

I turned around to see a tall woman, mid-twenties with red hair cascading down her shoulders. She had fine features and pale skin. She wore a turquoise and black choker necklace and a close-bodiced black dress. Her hands were clasped, fingers interlaced, in what seemed to be a pious gesture.

I blinked. "No, child, eet eez just the news," I said in my high-European accent, French and Russian with a dash of Castilian, which I cultivated for occasions such as these, and which seemed to necessitate a slight tightening of my nasal muscles. I lifted my nose and peered directly into the woman's eyes.

I wasn't sure about the *child* reference, but then decided that it sounded quite fitting, prayerful even. And the woman didn't flinch. "So many lost souls . . . " I continued in a ponderous voice. I forgot to use my accent, but waved my hands back and forth over the newspaper as if it were a Eucharistic offering.

The woman took a step toward me. She seemed to make a point of staring down at the open newspaper. Its bold-print heading was in full view:

PERSONAL ADS -

SATISFY YOUR NEED

I covered the print with my napkin.

The woman was carrying a gold-lamé bag, very bright, almost iridescent, and she wore matching gold pumps—a bit small it seemed, as her toes were visibly cramped inside the pointed tips of the shoes. I tried to change the subject. "Child, your gold shoes and gold bag, they're miraculous," I said. "Years ago, in the middle ages, they would have traded twenty horses for those shoes."

"Right now I'd trade them for *one* horse. I broke a heel. See?" She swiveled around and placed a hand against the wall. Then she bent over and held up her left foot for me to examine. I looked at the scuffed sole of the shoe and its missing heel, then contemplated the woman's supple calf. She bent over further, which pushed her hips toward me. "I'll have to call a taxi," she said.

Of course I had to be chivalrous, gentile, gallant. "Don't bother with that. Come, I'll give you a lift."

She stood up straight and turned to face me. "—But you're not even done with your coffee . . . "

I beckoned her closer, wagged my fingers until she leaned toward me. "Don't tell anyone, but this coffee isn't very good," I whispered. Then I winked. My wink is one of my best qualities. I know that.

The woman laughed loudly, belly-laughed—almost brayed, as if I had told a wonderful joke, or made a heavenly pun.

I was somewhat flattered, but wished that she would calm herself. Her guffaws made her seem coarse. Under the table, the newly-starched creases of my slacks itched against my thighs. I stood up and touched the woman's shoulder. "Come," I said, and took a step toward the door. The woman—minus one heel—hobbled and limped and then held onto my arm with two hands for support.

Outside, the sun was bright. It burst out of the sky

with an intensity that demanded sunglasses. From my jacket pocket, I slipped out my Ray-Ban Clubmasters. The woman leaned closer to me.

The car was a block away, near the cove where snorkelers traversed the kelp, and where last year a sixteen-year-old boy had cracked his head open on a submerged rock when he tried to dive into the water. My tan Alfa Romeo Duetto convertible was parked with the front wheels cranked against the curb, exposing their zigzag treads.

"Pretty fancy car for a priest," she said.

"It's an old car actually—1969. See the boat tail?" I pointed at the streamlined trunk of the car. "They don't make them like that anymore."

I opened the passenger door, and the woman got in. "You should have a customized license plate that says *CAR-4-GOD* or something . . . " She giggled. "My name is Luna. I suppose I should tell you that."

I sat in the driver's seat, turned the ignition, and released the handbrake. It wheezed, then snapped free. I shifted into first and pulled into the street. "I'm Father Franco," I said, with a heavily accented "a," like the third syllable in *Tutankhamen*.

"I know . . . " said Luna. She had a mysterious lilt in her voice—as if I ought to inquire how she gleaned this information; as if I ought to imagine that she was telepathic, or perhaps a witch. But I didn't respond. She continued, "You can just drop me off at the bus stop on Torrey Pines Road." She laid her head back on the seat, offering her face to the sun.

"Do you live far from there?" I checked the rearview mirror. No one was following us.

"I live on Mount Soledad. Behind the Cross, where the midgets live." She laughed and raised both hands above her knees. Then she touched my thigh with her left hand—just for a moment, a blazing burning moment; and it was as if that hand kept my leg from pressing down on the accelerator, as if my thigh muscle were paralyzed. The car slowed, lagged, and the RPMs dropped. Luna lifted her hand and immediately I downshifted and stepped on the gas. The car surged ahead.

"But you are not a *meejette*. Bless their souls," I said, careful to keep my accent. I looked again at Luna's profile, stared openly now: flawless skin, round lips, full figure. "You look quite . . . healthy."

"I live near the midget colony. You know there's a colony on the mountain, right?"

I didn't know. "Yes, I have heard thees."

"I'll show you their houses." She patted my shoulder, but these were short firm pats, as if reassuring an elderly dog. "Don't worry. Just keep going. Turn right at the next intersection. Then we'll go up."

She was quiet for a while, enjoying the sun. She unbuttoned the top of her dress, rubbed the tender, paper-white skin over her collarbone, and closed her eyes. I wondered when the last time was that she got any sun at all . . . We headed into a long incline in third gear, a slightly chugging ride which seemed to reanimate Luna. "Today is the first day!" she announced.

I didn't answer, stared straight at the road ahead. The slope was so steep and continuous that it appeared vertical and out of focus.

"Today is the first day, for three reasons." She spoke almost didactically now, over-enunciating the final syllables of her words. "Number one—I changed mascara. I switched to a lighter shade. The mouth and the eyes shouldn't fight each other for attention." She paused as if to assess my suspense regarding the presumably upcoming reasons two and three, but I kept watch on the whirring black asphalt ahead. My hands grasped the steering wheel at exactly the two and ten o'clock positions.

"Number two, I broke up with my boyfriend, Rex," she said matter-of-factly. "And number three . . . " Her voice trailed off again.

I pressed a toggle switch controlling an aftermarket windshield spray nozzle which I'd had specially installed, and set the wipers to work scraping away at a curious red stain in front of the rearview mirror. "What is number three?" I finally asked.

But Luna didn't hear, or pretended not to hear. She had grasped the mirror, turned it toward her, and began to examine her face, which seemed to entail hardening her features—firming her lips and narrowing her eyes like the angry heroine of rock music video, which I only happened to see on MTV *en passant*, switching the channels to BBC News. She ran two fingers down the curve of her jaw, under her chin, and down her neck. "Rex said my best feature is my throat, because it's long."

"Let's have no more of thees talk about Rex."

"So you want to know the third reason? Why today is the first day? I can tell you because you're a priest, right?"

I had to nod.

"I used to be, well, almost a sexual addict. I used to need it *a lot*. All the time, indoors, outdoors—especially outdoors." Here she spread her arms to indicate the grandiose nature of her sexual exploits in the wilderness, her communion with Isis, Astarte and Frey . . . Her hand grasped my thigh again. She left the hand there for a few minutes—five, fifteen, fifty, I wasn't sure—electric fingers, soft pressure. I could feel the tactile pads and the point where the fingers merged with her palm. I could feel her gently massaging me. "Today is the first day of my *second* virginity," said Luna. And abruptly, she withdrew her hand from my leg.

We drove for ten more minutes in silence until Luna said, "Turn here." I guided the car around a corner bordered on both sides by pine and scrub oak. "How do you do it, Franco—I mean *Father* Franco . . . How do you go without sex? I bet a lot of girls try to make you change your mind." She laughed and held up the pinky of her left hand and waived it in front of her, flexing it, as if that little finger itself might be a tiny female flying about in the throes of estrus, searching for a partner.

The road sloped sharply down. I shifted into second gear and the engine roared. The tachometer bounded up to 6500 RPMs. Then we swung through a true hairpin curve. The rear tires, vintage Pirellis, squealed and gripped the pavement. Luna was pinned by centrifugal force against the door. There was no need for directions. The road had become almost a single lane that twisted and cut its way up the mountain through a solid rock wall, which must have been blasted by dynamite, leaving jagged marks where it separated. On the other side of the road were an embankment of grass and flowers, and a steep cliff. Here and there, a house—or rather a bit of a house, a secluded porch or louvered window—exposed itself through the trees.

"What sign are you?" asked Luna, and then quickly cut herself off— "Oh, I forgot, that's forbidden. I don't want to get you excommunicated or anything."

"Actually, Vatican II does allow for certain forms of astrology," I replied. I had no idea whether or not this was correct.

The road ducked underneath a fairytale arched bridge, a cantilevered span of wood and trellis. Blackbirds dotted the bridge, and upon our approach they took off and flocked into the afternoon sky. We passed another house, closer to road. It did have a rather Lilliputian blue door, only about three feet tall, guarded by stone gargoyles and dangling vines. "See how tiny that door is? A midget lives there!" Luna whispered. She leaned closer until her mouth was almost touching my ear and I could smell her vanilla perfume. I could feel the heat of her breath. "They come out at night mostly. Mostly . . . "

I pulled the rearview mirror back into position. No one was following us. We drove further without talking. The steady hum of the motor was the only sound in the muggy air. For a few moments, a pair of writhing mating dragonflies—bodies coupled, pulsing abdomens, wings invisibly fast and in stroboscopic slow motion at once—wriggled around each other, caught in front of the window where the air pressure held them in a vacuum against the wiper blades. They copulated in suspended animation, perhaps in a time warp, and Luna couldn't take her eyes off them. I activated the wipers again and the soft rubber blades guided the insects off the windshield, above the chrome frame, and into the blue yonder. Luna turned—writhing herself—to watch the dragonflies disappear behind us. Then she gasped. "Stop! We're here."

But I didn't jam on the brakes. I slowed gently past a black metal gate. This one was unlocked and hanging open, yet wound in a frenzy of barbed wire surrounding and entombing what seemed to be pieces of bone. Luna wouldn't look at the gate. She leaned forward as if about to protest that I'd passed her house, but I shifted the car into reverse and backed up twenty feet until she said, "Park here." Then she bent down in her seat to gather up her gold bag which had tipped over, spilling its secret feminine contents. I caught a glimpse of a yellow hairbrush matted with red hair, a lipstick with its pink tongue exposed (which she quickly capped), tampons, several medication bottles (hardly reassuring), and a container of Tic-Tac breath mints. Without offering one to me, Luna poured out a few Tic-Tacs and popped them in her mouth. "You can come in if you'd like."

I shut off the engine. Then simultaneously both of us stared at a large gray rock on the other side of the road. It was a smooth, egg-shaped stone as big as a propane tank, adorned with a black spray-painted stenciled goat head. The paint looked fresh. Rivulets of spray dripped from the bottom of the goat's head, where its neck should be. "Your neighbors like art . . . " I said.

"This way," pointed Luna, and I followed her up a splintery wooden stairway. On the steps lay a trail of white and gray feathers. Caught in the railing were tufts of brownish fur with dried skin attached.

"Dog?" I asked.

"Don't worry, Wolfer's at the vet getting neutered." She laughed. "Do you think that will change his personality? He's very protective of me. But he likes to eat the neighbors' pets. He eats birds, too—I don't know how he catches them."

"Bad Wolfer," I said.

"Do you think that will change his personality?"

"What do you mean?"

She turned and glanced down at my genital area. "Snip-snip-snip . . . "

I blinked. "Slightly, perhaps." And then I didn't know what else to say. But it didn't matter because Luna opened the unlocked door and led me into her house. I felt a moment of hesitation, a visceral warning, but suppressed it and walked through the door into what was in fact a studio. There was very little furniture, only a metal bookshelf and a white plastic loveseat, the kind most people would have as garden furniture, positioned under the front window. Attached to the far wall was a tall black metal frame with handles on each side. It was a Murphy bed which swung down into place—or perhaps it was a body rack. On the left side of the studio was another window, which gave the impression of being opaque, as it was backed by pine branches pressed so close to the pane that the needles lay flat against the glass like green hair. Window hair.

"Would you like a drink?" asked Luna, somewhat mechanically, with one hand resting on her hip. "I have coffee and tea as well if you prefer."

"Maybe a brisk cup of tea. For thee mountain

curves."

She turned toward the kitchen, walking much more gracefully now, despite the missing heel. She left me to amuse myself in the living room while she made tea. The plastic loveseat was covered in pillows, but looked uncomfortable nonetheless. I chose to survey the bookshelf instead. It was rather sparse. On the bottom shelf were two *Architectural Digest* magazines, a Gideon's Bible, and a *Victoria's Secret* catalog. On the middle shelf lay a Swiss Army knife and a dog-eared copy of *PLAYGIRL* with an oiled insectoid-muscled blond übermensch on the cover, staring out with a salacious smirk. I averted my eyes. On the top shelf were an old pocket watch, a bottle of suntan lotion, and an antique hard-backed volume: Nikolai Gogol, *Dead Souls*. I flipped open the cover. On the title page, in round bubble-lettered printing, were three words, written in a peculiar position:

NEMESIS

FECUND

I
N
C
A
R
N
A
D
I
N
E

My palms began to itch and I rubbed them together. If anyone looked at me, would they think I was praying?

In the kitchen, Luna was patting tea into an infusion machine. She had removed her gold shoes, which now lay one on top of the other against the wall. I could see the profile of her upper body. Again, I was taken by the smoothness of her gait. She seemed to float back and forth.

Luna came out of the kitchen carrying a serving tray with a glass teapot, two hexagonal cups (pink and black), a pitcher of cream, and a flask with rolled cinnamon protruding out of the tap. She sat down on the plastic loveseat. "Take off your jacket and relax," she said, patting the seat beside her invitingly. I laid my jacket over the arm of the couch and sat down, crossing one priest-worthy black pant leg over the other. I took the black cup that she held out for me, slipping my fingers under hers through the handle. For a moment, our hands touched, and she gazed into my eyes. "This was Rex's—my boyfriend's—favorite cup."

I lifted the glass, felt the tea steam under my nose and the vapors in my beard. I brought the cup to my mouth, pressed one blazing hot hexagonal corner against my bottom lip and slurped out some tea.

"No . . . " Luna giggled, leaning into me. I felt the warmth of her body. "Silly, you have to press your mouth on the flat part of the cup, on the side. Don't they teach priests how to drink?" She rested a hand on my knee as I tried another sip. "Rex did that the first time he drank from the cup, too. I had to teach him not to burn his tongue."

"Now let's have no more of thees talk about Rex. Remember, you are in your second—" and then I knew I shouldn't say it. I hesitated. My chest tightened. *Virginity* spoken by a priest really applied to the immaculate conception of the Virgin Mary, right? But I had to say something. "You are in your second . . . *period.*" Not much better. I coughed, sat forward, and tried to gulp down some more tea. It seared my throat.

Luna let out a deep sigh and lay her head on my shoulder. I had to be careful not to spill tea in her hair. She held out one hand and brought it up toward my chin. Then she touched the underside of my goatee, right at the point where the shaved hair of the beard met the skin of my throat. "I've always been fascinated by beards," she said. "I always wondered about the bottom of the beard. How far in does it go?" She had a glazed look in her eyes as she traced the line of my beard from one side to the other and back, stroking the hairline softly.

I shivered and sat very still.

With her finger still under my chin, in the sensitive V of the jawbone, she giggled. And then she blushed again. "Your beard, at the edge, it feels kind of like after a bikini wax, and . . . " Now she was laughing like a schoolgirl, leaning into me again. "Ohhh," she purred, "I feel like I can tell you anything. Just anything. It's like we're on the same wavelength." Her eyes gleamed. "I know, Father, think of a color."

"Pardon?"

"You think of a color. Just close your eyes and think of it, and telepathically I'll be able to guess."

I did close my eyes. Not because I was playing along, but because I suddenly felt weary—no, drunk, actually. But I only had tea . . . And since the thought was still in my mind, I did happen to think of a color, jet black, which kept being interrupted by red. All of a sudden Luna was in my lap— kissing me—two hands on my cheeks, her fingers sliding over my ears and though my hair. I tried to lean away, but I was flat against the wall and my head hit the windowsill. Then I didn't want to lean away. Softly, I placed my hands on Luna's shoulders, allowing them to caress her arms, her back—but not venture in front or below her waist. A priest's hands couldn't go below the waist, right? Not at first . . .

My tenderness seemed only to inflame Luna. Her kisses became hard and aggressive. She squirmed in my lap and pressed her lips against mine with such force that our teeth collided—I could hear them clack. She grabbed my hand and guided it under her brassiere.

Outside, there was a sound of rustling leaves, snapping twigs, and a wolfish snarl. I turned my head up toward the window and, out of peripheral vision, saw a streak of red at the edge of the curtain, then an eyebrow and an eye peering into the bottom corner. There was another snarl, almost a choke. A very loud pounding, like sonic booms, resounded on the outer wall of the house. The couch trembled. The window shuddered. I cringed, ready for the glass to explode on my scalp.

Luna froze, dead still in my arms. Even her lips, interlocked with mine, were motionless, except for pulsing tendrils of nerves.

"LUNA!" A huge voice bellowed from outside. "LUNA!" The voice was lower now, almost hoarse.

She began to quiver, first her cheeks, then her whole body. "Oh my God! It's Rex!" she hissed.

There was a final tremendous pound on the door—as from a battering ram or an immense combat boot, and the door crashed open. There stood Rex. All six-foot-eight of him. His huge muscles rippled under a red tank top. He was enormous, obviously a weightlifter. His exercise shorts glistened with sweat. His back muscles, latissimus dorsi, bulged under his arms. His nose protruded like a falcon beak. His eyes were a sharp, crystalline blue. And I realized that I was staring at the same face posted on the cover of Luna's *PLAYGIRL* magazine.

"Luna," growled Rex, who spoke with some sort of German or Austrian accent, an authentic accent. "Luna, I toald you I'd be here ot eight!" He took a step toward us, a giant menacing step, and glared at me. "Who ze fock eez zees?"

Luna was up instantly, pressing two hands on Rex's gargantuan chest, which seemed as futile as trying to hold back a rhinoceros. Rex took another step forward, plowing Luna in front of him. He stood directly in line with the door now, blocking my only escape. "Sone-ahv-a-beetch priest!" His accent distorted the words, made them even more jagged and sinister. He had a massive fist, held it in front of a bulging forearm.

I thought of martyred saints, impaled shaven monks, and oddly, Saint Agatha—whose breasts were cut off as punishment.

"NO!" shrieked Luna. "DON'T! Please, I love you, Rex!" She embraced him and began kissing his steroidal neck, which had a thick tendon running down the side like a water hose. "No," she pleaded again, crying now, both her legs wrapped around the steeled quadriceps of his thigh.

I saw a flash of light, a beam from the open door, and I knew the time had come, like a parting of the Red Sea or a respite between hordes of descending locusts. I jumped to my feet and ran—lurched really—past the hulking Rex and the trembling Luna. He tried to wrench free of her to grab me, but she held onto his arm and was lifted from the ground. I rushed past Rex and only his elbow touched me, but I felt his stinging hot perspiration on my skin and smelled his odor. Then I was out the door—safe in the air, safe by a hair, a miracle, a sanctification. I dashed down the wooden stairs, which seemed more rickety than before. A clump of the brown fur had come loose. It floated in the air, then clung to my leg like a parasite.

Finally, breathing heavily, I was in my car. I was surprised, astonished, not to see the monstrosity Rex bounding after me, grabbing the bumper and lifting the rear wheels up, or groaning and heaving rocks like Goliath. But none of these things occurred. Rex didn't even emerge from the house.

I was perspiring now. The leather-sheathed car key almost slipped out of my hand. At last, I managed to insert the key and turn the ignition. The car started immediately—a divine occurrence itself. I screeched out a three-point turn on the little road, jamming and grinding the gear box. Then I saw it! I slammed on the brakes. My heart pounded. On top of the rock with the stenciled goat head stood a very short man—a midget, a dwarf, a troll in a black gown—posed rigidly like a grotesque statuette. He was barefoot, with very big feet given his stature. He held a long red candle in one hand; in the other, he grasped a human skull.

The midget had a pointed goatee. He threw back his head to look at the moon, barely visible in the evening sky. Then he lowered his glance to stare at me with an expression of pure disdain, bordering on disgust. His eyes were open but impenetrable, emitting a tenebrous shadowy light. Still holding my gaze, in a motion which seemed deliberately slow, he brought the candle to his lips and blew out the flame.

The faux-priest collar tightened around my throat, chafed, and bit into my skin. I reached to tug away the fabric, stretching it out, pulling harder and harder with a fierce grasp—until the collar ripped free and hung down over my bare chest.

Atop the rock, arms held straight out from his body now so his caftan sleeves hung and fluttered like wings, the midget laughed at me . . .

ERRED

It started in the closet.

The closet was supposed to help. It was a sanctuary away from the light. Not just a normal light—a 2,000-watt, 3.5-million-candlepower halogen beast in the atrium that illuminated, irradiated everything within a perimeter of 50 yards, down to ground zero. It pierced through the Levelor® blinds and seared into my room. I tried towels, thick all-cotton beach towels—huge things folded double, Sears Best Quality imported from Brazil (Quetzalcoatl Comfort Plus™), hooked with syringe-needled drapery hangers, curved four-inch spikes thrust deep into the fleshy cotton. I strung them to cover all of my windows in the low-budget studio near Doggie Beach. An insulating fabric, an isolating tactic to sequester myself.

But the light curved around the top of the window frames and arced under the towels, sliced in through the door and cut a beaded insidious line across the rug—into my head, through my eyelids, torching my face so I wouldn't sleep, even with the pillow crushed around my face and a dirty T-shirt knotted over my brow.

Then I moved into the closet.

Some apartments have tiny square-shaped closets, toilet-sized really, only enough room for a short pole the size of a baseball bat. Not mine. In fact, when I first rented, the closet had been one of the best features of the apartment, an allure like a glinting gold watch—that, and the fact there was a skylight in the bathroom so you could see the birds, before they died. "Nice big closet . . . " my grandmother had said. Then she smelled inside the oven and opened the ice cube box in the freezer where the last tenant had left some gray cubes.

My closet was long, so when I tugged out the dresser and threw my trash bag full of socks on top, and pulled out the tennis racket that I hadn't used in two years, and found the brown sack with six extra tubes of Shoe Goo® in it, and wheeled out my new 270V K-Mart HEPA vacuum cleaner with the suction massage attachment set, and picked up my briefcase of relaxation tapes from K-Tel Inc., with the voice of the woman who talked like she was breathing, and breathed like she was talking to the sea . . . When I tossed all this into the center of the room, there was a fine place to sleep inside the closet. A good dark place when you slid closed the door. A nice private place, like a tent, a trunk, or a womb—it's sick to think of a coffin, though.

I folded the comforter, all white as I liked, first in half, in fourths—no fifths, exactly—just the right width to wedge in place. I slid in the single-width futon covered with sheets. I shut the wooden fan-folding door so it was dark. Pitch dark. Utter dark. You couldn't see a fist in front of your face. I hoped it was dark enough to sleep. Just a wink, a nod or two. A gasp or three. A wince in the night.

But then I couldn't breathe. The closet smell, enclosed and caustic, dusty and barbed, would suffocate all, even me. So I slept on the bedroom floor, between the socks and the Shoe Goo® that had oozed out of its tubes. My head rested near the relaxation tapes that never worked.

I smelled it in the morning, deep in my sinus passages and nasal pores, cilial hair clotted, burning, dripping, sneezing—93% fluids, of which the body is composed. Then coughing, hacking, hawking, wheezing sternutation. Face-fiery allergy that would drive a cat to water, drive water from a cat, out of its fur . . . I could *feel* the stench, the camphored wooden odor, the effluvium of spores wafting around my head, diving into my skin and down my throat. And so I sniffed— a sniff detector, Inspector Detector—through a clogged nose and itching eyes with sleepies at the corners.

They lived in the wood. That I determined. Not in the finished wood on the outside, but in the porous composite wood on the insides of the shelves; in the interior, that's where they gathered—mold particles. Mildew spicules. Most likely some had dried and floated now, colonies suspended in the evil light, actually worse in their fatal nimbus. They whirled and flowed, dived and careened into my scalp to sicken me. I blew my nose again and again, then opened the extra box of Kleenex™ brand unscented facial tissues, two-ply, yellow, red with blood, watered by sneeze.

I tugged out the dresser, a thrift-shop item, $35 for the last owner's bad karma, karmic specter, drawer-dwelling scourge, hell-bent on anaphylaxis; stirring my thyroids, adenoids, calling forth pruritus, which is really just a lower degree of pain, they say. A bright red rash with curious carmine spots flowered across my forehead, on my hands, wrists, ankles, and bare feet.

At the techno-store, the gadget place, the you-didn't-know-you-needed-it mart (I knew; I had the catalog), The Sharper Image, I walked up to an effete salesman whose hair was razor-cut, whose face was skin-balmed with lotion for men, I'm sure. He looked at me with some disdain, nose lifted, thin-lipped arrogance really, while I blew into my crumpled napkin, the one with golden arches that thank-the-great-Western-God I had the wisdom to save after a McFishwich™ at American's finest. So Mr. Techno Effete was watching me in my old tennis shoes, Elevator Shoes® (but you couldn't tell, right?), and my size 38 regular shorts (slightly stained around the crotch), and my JCP dragon polo shirt. He was smirking and primping in the side mirror (he thought I couldn't see), until I pulled out my American Express Green Card and bought without question the Sonic Breeze™ Air Purifier/Ionizer, the Boldus® Modular Ion Sphere, the Teledyne Sequencing Humidifier Unit, and a pair of Comforting Blue-Gel Insoles in clear plastic. CAUTION GEL POISON: DO NOT EAT.

Back at my car, I immediately slipped the Gel insoles into my shoes and squished my foot against the accelerator. I got home quickly, and the wood odor burned my face. I gasped and tried not to inhale, held my breath—tremors of temple and bursting lungs . . . I ripped open the boxes to hook up the machines for my perfect atmosphere, like the cult fascists in *Biosphere II*. Even better! I dumped water into the Sequencing Humidifier and turned on the Modular Ion Sphere and connected the Air Purifier. When I did all that and still smelled mephitis, without a blink, I emptied the cabinet: old polyester boxers, an unused twelve-pack of condoms, a pile of snaking belts. I dragged the whole thing, first the frame, then the drawers, three-at-a-time out into the street, leaving a path of splinters that shone crystal clear in broad daylight. I hauled the cabinet out to the great bin of the trash and left it there. Probably an expensive piece of furniture to begin with. The foragers no doubt knew, ten minutes later, when they put it in their van and drove away.

Inside my room, now more vacant, cleansed of tainted air, purified from within and without like a newborn babe, a wriggling calf—THE STENCH WAS STILL THERE! God Damn It! So I shut off the Sequencing Humidifier. Did water vapor make the mold grow? Nurture it? Feed it? Expand it? I got down on hands and knees and smelled the rug, the petroleum-based textile fibers, rust-colored, filthy, but no real odor . . . For good measure, I threw out the mattress, a green flowered thing, Sealy Posturepedic™ (no telling what was inside: body exoderm, exodus, detritus, mellitus); I dragged that out to the bin too, only chafing it at the bottom. Again, the trash hunters were soon satisfied.

Opening the windows didn't help. It made things worse, even with the throbbing Ion Sphere on "MAX" and the Air Purifier on "THRUST." My throat was raw, cheeks inflamed, eyes itching, vision glazed. With streaming nose. I sniffed around like a dog, then finally took a scalding shower under the Rain Bird® Shower Massage, jetting water over my eyelids and into my mouth, curbing my sneeze and frenzy of itch for a few moments. But when I stepped out, I coughed again and burned some more, then went back in for a 49-minute shower—to hell with conservation, I needed H_2O.

Then I took the pills. A triple-dose of Claritin®

(Loratadine), the allergy medicine that makes you sleep although they say it won't . . . And I drank a bottle of organic Fraise™ wine (no sulphites) that tasted like rotting fruit. And made me vomit.

Sleep is by no means a respite, you know. I tossed and trembled, and rolled and coughed some more. The pillowcase had a scarlet cloud. The tissues were gone. The sky was dark. The wood-stink surrounded me. Where was it coming from? Dear Christ . . . In the closet doors! In between the lattice—oh, so subtle. That's where the mold must hide, in compressed and flaked yeasty particles. So I ripped out the doors, broke them out of their tracks, flung them out the door and smelled a new a pungent sickly scent, on my arms, in my hair, on my cheeks . . .

Even with a wash, a scrubbing rub, a savage abrading, the stink wouldn't leave. It was in my body now, I could tell. It was not merely in the wood. Or perhaps . . . And I closed my eyes. Perhaps. And I tried not to think of it. Maybe the smell was my own? The allergen, my skin . . . The effluvium, my hair . . .

I sniffed a finger, just a test, a thumb no less, and coughed again in a burst from my abdomen. I grit my teeth. "People Allergic to Themselves." I had seen the episode on *Oprah*, after she gained back the weight.

In the night, out in the street, alone on the corner with no escape, diseased by my own body, my essence, my sheer corporeality. There was no outlet, no egress, no relief.

At Doggie Beach on the sand, with clots of canine feces sticking to my shoes, I waded into the ocean. First to the thighs, then moving in, water lapping at my chest . . . Saltwater cures and stings the nostrils. It burns the rash where you have scrubbed thousands of times. It mats the hair inside your nose. But it floats the worry out to sea.

Stroke by stroke, in the dark, through the depths, shoes kicked to the bottom long ago, shirt undone and slowly released—it clung at the wrist and finally gave in, hovering, undulating and waving, fluttering and mocking under the moon. Far, far out, well past the pier, so the shoreline was gone and the city lights were just a glow, an iridescence after the bomb. Kicking more, kicking free. Aching legs and tired back—a sneeze no less, in the fucking sea!

In my pocket, safe in their foil, in their plastic, pre--molded and tested, the Claritin® pills that make you drowsy and clog your mind as well. Twelve to a sheet in a Press-Tab-Saver™—I took fourteen, gulping them in, saltwater for drink, brine for taste, marine microbes to follow.

Many gulps, treading water, heavy head, circling arms. Sharp pains in my spine. Neck up, neck down. Neck up, neck down. A cortisol sputter in flexed fingers. Homeo-adrenaline fights "Active Ingredient: Chlorpheniramine Maleate™" and loses. Allergy medicine, exponent fourteen, plus the seven before.

And then the sleeping pills. DOZE-AID® (Doxylamine), from SuperValue, Inc. I had these, too. A bottle of twenty. Down the throat. Through the esophagus. Into the stomach. Activated by saline and dissolved by HCL. The man-made vice will always win . . .

Then I let my eyelids close, the way they wanted. And let my arms sink in, the way they needed. And felt the warm water in my ears. Once again, I opened my eyes. Just once more.

I thought I saw it. I knew I felt it—the giant dark form lurking beneath. Pulsing below. Cold . . . Cold and wet.

REFRACTION

Thoren pushed the "Play" button and tried not to tremble. There was a thirty-second lead-time before the CD would start. He lifted the comforter, slid between the sheets, and switched off the bed lamp. He pressed down with his toes, and the sheets and blankets slid from under the mattress. Then he lifted his legs and swung them up until the sheets were tucked around his feet, the way liked. He clasped his hands over his chest and took deep steady breaths, pushing out his diaphragm with each inhalation. The CD started. A lyrical woman's voice spoke: "Hello, my friend . . . You are warm and safe. You are relaxed. You can hear water gently lapping. You are happy. You feel warm and safe. Close your eyes. You are at peace . . . "

Thoren shuddered when his dog, a plump white Bichon Frise named "Rufus," sprang up on his stomach and barked. "Rufus, can't you see I'm trying to relax here? Go away," said Thoren. But he didn't push the dog away, and Rufus didn't leave.

The CD continued. "You are in a quiet place where it is dark and secure. You breathe deeply and regularly. You are warm and comfortable . . . " Rufus had crawled up near Thoren's neck and, using his hind feet for leverage, was trying to dig his way under the covers. His feathery tail flicked against Thoren's cheek.

"That's enough," said Thoren. "You're going into the kitchen." He grasped the dog with both hands under its front legs, and swung out of bed.

The voice kept speaking. "You are alone and wonderfully relaxed. No one will disturb you."

"Yeah, sure," said Thoren. Guided by a glowing LED light, he switched off the CD player's power button with his toe. It was stupid of him to have sent away for the *Sensual Sleep* CD in the first place. Fifteen dollars, Christ . . .

Thoren couldn't seem to find the hall light switch so he walked slowly toward the kitchen, taking tiny steps, dangling Rufus in front of him. Small particles, crumbs and dust stuck to the sales of his feet. He had forgotten to sweep. He kicked open the kitchen door and turned on the light with his elbow. A large cockroach scuttled across the floor and collided with the counter. Rufus saw the bug too, barked twice, and twisted out of Thoren's arms to chase it.

"Catch it, Rufus! Eat!" Thoren stamped his foot. "We don't want any pests here. We don't need that."

Thoren walked back to the bedroom, but he knew he

wouldn't sleep. It was only ten o'clock. Most people were still awake, reading, watching TV, or relaxing with their families. He would just lie down again to try and rest. Then he changed his mind. He opened the window shade. Gingerly, he slid the dust cover off his telescope and patted the shiny white tube. He had sent away for the scope from a JCPenney catalog: "Enjoy the Universe with this High Power Astronomer's Telescope!" He had installed the telescope himself. Half of the eight-inch-diameter refractive tube was inside his room under the open window, and the other half stuck out over the fire escape. Outside, in front of the telescope, hung a golden pathos plant with an array of heart-shaped leaves, so no one would see the telescope during the day. Like a secret agent, Thoren could raise and lower the plant by means of a pulley attached to the fire escape and a rope which led from the plant pot into his room. He was very proud of this arrangement.

Thoren bent to focus the view finder. His favorite subject was a young woman across the street. Sometimes she undressed without closing her drapes. Using the bottom of his pajama shirt, Thoren dusted off the eyepiece. He heard his own heavy mouth-breathing, so he forced his breaths through his nose. He tugged on the rope. A branch of the plant, crooked and withered, caught on the front of the telescope. Thoren yanked the rope and the plant jerked up—but the branch broke off. It hung, swaying on the end of his telescope, covering the lens.

"Shit," said Thoren. He had to go out onto the fire escape to move the branch.

As Thoren stuck his head outside the window, the night air stung his cheek. But the cold was exciting somehow, invigorating. His shoulders tingled. With one knee on the window sill, he wriggled out onto the fire escape. He was afraid of heights and tried not to look down—four stories was a long way . . . But he couldn't resist and gazed down at the street, empty except for a few parked cars. The view was almost desolate. Then Thoren saw someone: a man who had been crouching behind one of the cars scurried over to another car and crouched down again. In his hand he held a tool, a thin metal strip, and stuck it between the window and door of a car, slid it around, back and forth—suddenly, he looked up. The man's eyes met Thoren's. They stared at each other. Thoren shivered—maybe the guy had a gun . . .

But the man didn't seem to be aggressive. In fact, he was looking up at Thoren in a friendly way, like a comrade . . . My God, thought Thoren, he assumes I'm a thief, too. He thinks I'm part of his thieving brotherhood. Thoren clenched his fist. "POLICE!" He shouted down. "NINE-ONE-ONE!" His voice cracked.

The man took off running. Soon he was disappearing into the night. Thoren laughed. "And don't come back." But by then the man was out of sight.

Across the street, a light went on. Thoren grabbed the

branch off the telescope, clamped it between his teeth, and climbed back into his room. The apartment now felt hot. His chest felt tight. He was wheezing and the branch had left a bitter taste in his mouth, but he didn't take off his shirt and rub in Mentho-Lyptus ointment. He didn't gargle with Listerine. He bent down to look through his telescope. With moist fingers, he adjusted the focus knob, panning over the brick building across the street—cable TV wires coating the exterior like spider web strands, crumbling mortar, a window frame—There she was! His favorite girl. And she was getting undressed! Thoren could see her blond hair and her back. She reached and pulled off her sweater. "Yes . . . " said Thoren. She started to undo her brassiere. "Oh yes . . . " he sighed. But the woman hesitated. She stood perfectly still with one hand on her bra strap. For some reason, Thoren thought she had heard him. His cheeks flushed. Then she switched off her light, and the view became too dim to make out much detail.

Thoren decided he was hungry. He went to make some hot milk and eat a fig. While the milk simmered, he took out his bag of figs and counted them. "Eight," he said out loud. "Eight figs." He pinched one out of the bag and bit off its stem, spitting it across the room toward the trash. It landed on the floor. Thoren didn't pick it up. "Rufus, fig stem . . . " he called in a lilting voice. Rufus wasn't in the kitchen anymore. Thoren poured his milk and started to eat the fig, brought it to his lips—and gagged. The fig caught dangled between his teeth. As he stared down, it looked like a turtle without a shell, a globular body packed with hundreds of gooey seeds inside—eggs. Thoren wrapped the fig in a napkin and left it on the counter. He sipped his hot milk, slurped it, but then a knock sounded on the door. Must be next door, he figured. But the knocking grew louder. Incessant. Three raps, a pause, three more. The pounding came unmistakably from his door. Thoren twitched. He rarely had visitors.

He tip-toed over to the door and peered through the peephole. Outside stood a boy about eleven years old, wearing a safari hat. Around his neck hung a pair of binoculars. The boy knocked again. "Who is it?" asked Thoren, in his roughest voice.

"Michael from across the street," the boy answered. "I want to see your telescope."

"I, I don't have a telescope."

"I know you have one," said Michael. "I watch you use it with my binoculars when I'm not watching pigeons."

Thoren stood perfectly still. He pretended he was dead. Maybe the boy would just leave.

Michael knocked again, his fist magnified through peephole. "I didn't tell my Dad about the telescope—yet . . . " Now Michael was jumping up to try and see into the peep-hole, and when Thoren opened the door, the boy almost fell in.

"Michael, it's illegal to spy on people without their

permission." Thoren said.

"Then how come you always look at my sister?"

"I do *not*," said Thoren, with a good rasp on "not." Maybe he could scare the boy away.

"My Dad always gets mad when guys look at my sister."

Thoren felt numb.

"Come on, I want to see your telescope."

"All right. Well, just for a moment. I'm very busy you know." He would just let the kid in for a minute.

Michael stepped into the apartment and walked directly toward Thoren's room. He must have known the telescope was on that side of the apartment. Thoren noticed the boy carried a walkie-talkie in his hand, a cheap plastic one. "That thing's not on, is it?" Thoren pointed.

"No. It's just for emergencies."

"Aren't you scared barging into someone's apartment who you don't even know? I could be a murderer, or a *molester* . . . "

Michael ignored him. Thoren blinked. His stomach burned. No one ever too him seriously . . . He stood still, undecided for a moment. But then Michael clicked on the walkie-talkie and a burst of crackling static shot out, surprisingly loud. Michael laughed.

"Okay, okay—here's the lens," Thoren pointed.

Michael shut off the walkie-talkie and gazed down, concentrating.

Thoren rushed his words. "I can change lenses, up to 1000 MX magnification. And this is the secret plant, see? I can pull it up with this rope."

"Can I look?"

It was a bad idea to let the boy look, Thoren knew it, but no one had ever seen it before. And Michael was so interested. "Well just for a second."

Michael squinted through the view-finder and swung the scope back and forth. "Wow. Cool . . . " Thoren was very pleased. Then Michael inhaled sharply. "Hey! There's my sister's room. I knew you looked at her."

"All right, enough with the telescope. You'd better go, now."

"Can I look just a little longer?"

"No."

Thoren pushed in front of the boy to slide on the telescope cover. Then Rufus trotted into the bedroom. "You have a puppy!" said Michael.

"Do I?"

"He looks like a snowball. Is his name *Snowball*?"

"No. *Rufus*."

Michael bent down to pet Rufus, who jumped up on his hind legs and sniffed and licked at Michael's hand. His ears fluttered up and down. "He likes me."

"He's hungry."

"Can I pick him up?"

Thoren nodded and Michael picked up the dog, which

whimpered and licked his face.

"Let's get him some dinner," said Michael. With confident steps, as if he had lived in the apartment for years, Michael strode into the hall, found the kitchen and gazed around, appraising it. Thoren's cup of warm milk was on the counter, and he poured it into the dog bowl. Rufus wiggled out of Michael's arms to lap up the milk.

"He puts his whole face in the bowl," said Michael. "See, his cheeks are wet!" Michael bent to pet Rufus on the top of his head, the dry part. Rufus rolled his head back and forth, almost dazed. He didn't seem to know whether to lift his head for petting, or put his head down to drink. Michael petted him a little more, then with his index fingers, he pulled up Rufus's ears and held them out from his head. "Airplane ears . . . Whshshshshshshsh."

"All right, let him drink now."

"I'm thirsty too," said Michael. "Do you have any apple juice?"

"Maybe."

"Well, if you have some, I'd like a bit."

"Please . . . " prompted Thoren.

"Please."

Thoren took out a cup and filled it with apple juice, pouring from an old plastic milk carton which he used to mix frozen concentrate. Michael gulped his juice, then glanced up. "How old are you?"

"Fifty-eight," answered Thoren. There was no harm

in telling his age, right?

"Don't you have a girlfriend?"

"Not right now." Thoren cleared his throat.

"Is that why you always look at my sister?"

Thoren flexed his fingers—he decided not to respond. He would just ignore the brat.

"I have a girlfriend," said Michael.

"Oh, do you?"

"Her name is Deena. Deena Peterson. She has diabetes."

Suddenly Thoren's neck was hot, searing. He was angry with the boy—angry about threatening to tell his father about the telescope, teasing with the walkie-talkie, bragging about his girlfriend. "DEENA PETIES—*DIABETIES* . . . DEENA PETIES—*DIABETIES* . . . " taunted Thoren, wiggling his head and torso.

Michael stared down at the floor and was quiet for a while. He set his empty apple juice glass on the counter. "That wasn't very nice."

Thoren pointed at the sink. "We wash our glasses here."

Michael turned on the faucet and rinsed his cup. The walkie-talkie was stuffed safely in the boy's back pocket—good. He set the glass rim-down in the dish drainer. Then he blinked. "What's that?" Michael waved a finger at the clotted, napkin-wrapped fig on the counter.

"Oh, that's just trash," said Thoren.

"We throw our trash in the bin."

There was silence for a long moment. "I think I'd better go now," said Michael. "Thank you for showing me the telescope."

"You're welcome." Thoren forced a smile and tapped on the boy's safari hat. "Don't forget your hat."

But Michael didn't smile. He grasped the brim with both hands and pulled it further down his scalp. He paced toward the door. Thoren opened it and Michael started to walk away—on an impulse, Thoren called to him, and his voice resounded in the empty hall. "Michael . . . "

The boy turned around.

"I'm sorry for what I said about Deena."

Michael's expression didn't change.

"Stop back some time. We'll look at the telescope again." Thoren realized his voice sounded anxious. So he coughed.

Michael walked down the stairs.

Thoren went over to the railing and looked down at the boy, watching his safari hat descend until it was just a small circle on the bottom floor. Then he went back into his apartment.

"Here, Rufus . . . " called Thoren. His throat was dry. He coughed again. Rufus came running and Thoren picked him up, curling the dog into his arms and under his chin. Milk from Rufus' wet cheeks dripped on Thoren's neck, but he didn't care, "Good Rufus," said Thoren. He stroked dog's soft furry head.

Safe in his room again, Thoren turned on the CD. "You are so, so comfortable," came the woman's voice. "It feels good to breathe. You are snug and warm. You are resting in a cloud, a warm billowy cloud. And there are no worries at all . . . "

Then Thoren switched out the light.

FISSION

When I move the brushes in circles, it sounds like rain. The metal strands swish and patter on top of the snare drum. It's a cloudburst on a tin roof, a staccato shower of raindrops in perfect rhythm with the piano. Pee Wee, the piano player, sits on the edge of the bench as he improvises. He holds out his elbows and raises his palms above the keys as if he is about to capture them in his bony white fingers. When the melody reaches a crescendo, I hit the high-hats or punch the bass. I'm the drum man.

During a break, the waitress Shirley comes over to me and I try to act nonchalant. "Hey Drum Man, have a drink," says Shirley. She smiles. Her skin is deeply tanned. There are freckles on her chest, which you can see because the top three buttons of her dress aren't fastened. "Come on, a big guy like you needs a drink." She rubs my forearm. Her hands are soft.

"Drum Man doesn't drink," says Fritz. His lips are always moist, even when he isn't holding his trumpet.

"Drum Man doesn't drink—he just eats . . . " Fritz laughs. His laugh is too high, really. It's almost a bleat. He pulls up his pants, which are already hiked above his navel, but he tugs them up even more so the fabric is tight against his crotch. Then he thrusts his pelvis forward. "Shirley babe, get me a gin-and-tonic, huh?" he says.

Shirley is rubbing my back now and automatically I suck in my stomach. "Sure you don't want anything?" she asks. I can smell her perfume. She smells sweet, like a fruit-and-coconut scented candle. In the dim light of the club, her eyes shine.

Above me dangles a shellacked swollen puffer fish almost two feet long. Its skin is ridged with spines. Its teeth are fanged. On the wall across the room hang two taxidermy swordfish posed face to face so their spears touch. A saltwater tank containing a small octopus and a rock sits near the window. When the club is crowded, the octopus gets nervous and squirts out its ink. But this late, the place is almost empty. It's 2:30 am already. We played six sets. My eyes burn from smoke in the bar, but I'm not tired. I'm never tired after playing. I keep the energy going. I'm the drum man.

Fritz walks over with a drink in his left hand. His right hand is tucked in his back pocket. "You played good tonight, man. Solid . . . " he says. "Maybe we'll keep you on." He pulls the hand out of his back pocket and pokes me in the stomach. I'm embarrassed by the way his fingers slip into the soft flesh of my middle. The heat rises in my cheeks. But I don't tell Fritz that he's an asshole. It's his gig, and he splits the cash four ways straight each week.

The drum set isn't mine. I don't have my own set, just some sticks and a practice block at home. But I have good sticks from Italy. *Dolce Ducto* brand, made of pear wood. The other musicians are putting away their instruments—Pee Wee unplugs his cords, zips up his electric keyboard; Fritz pulls off his mouthpiece and blows into it backward so the saliva drips out the metal rim and onto the floor. I just slide my drum sticks into my pocket.

The bar door opens and I can see Pacific Coast Highway, almost empty except for a few cars at the Stop-N-Go market and a motorcycle outside Ray's Handguns. The door stays ajar. I wonder if it's being held open by the wind. Then, in walks Juice.

I've never talked to him. He doesn't seem to like jazz. Shirley never introduced me, but I know Juice is her boyfriend, all six-foot-five of him. He's blond, broad-shouldered, with a page-boy haircut in the standard surf fashion. I've seen him three times and he is always wearing the same black T-shirt with a "Mr. Zog's Sex Wax" emblem. I wonder if the shirt is part of a set, or just washed frequently.

Juice sits down at a table near the door and takes a can of Heineken beer out of his pocket. Shirley doesn't say hello to Juice. His gaze follows her around the bar as she wipes down the tables. From a small refrigerator near the cash register, Shirley brings out some raw hamburger meat, squeezes it into a slot on top of the octopus tank, and watches as the creature scuttles out from behind its rock, tucks the meat in two tentacled legs, and opens its beak.

Then Shirley brings out the vacuum. It is a commercial unit the size of a lawn tractor. She turns on the machine and tugs it over to the area where Juice sits. Still, she hasn't said hello to him. The machine roars to life and Shirley works at the floor, pushing the head of the vacuum closer and closer to Juice until it bumps into his shoes and he is forced to raise his feet while she vacuums under his table. Then, with no further attention to other areas of the rug, Shirley drags the vacuum cleaner back into the closet and walks directly over to me. "Hey, Drum Man," she says. Her eyes widen and sparkle. "Juice and I are goin' to the beach. You wanna come?"

Juice makes a snorting noise. But it's Fritz who speaks. "Aw, Drum Man doesn't like the beach. When he was little, the kids called him *Whale-rus*. That's how he got into music, right?"

I stare at Fritz's small face. His skin is stretched tight so his eyes protrude like those of a rodent, a ferret or a vole. But Shirley is tickling my ear. She pulls on my earlobe playfully. She winks and her eyes sparkle even more. Suddenly—although I do hate the beach, and I know that Shirley is just using me to get back at her boyfriend, and Juice looks about as happy to have me along as to have a urethrectomy—in spite of all this, I find myself nodding. "Okay, Shirl," I say. And with my left hand, behind the wall partition so Juice can't see, I touch the small of her warm, curved back.

Juice drives an orange jeep with enormous tires. Stenciled on the doors in dripping black paint are the words "OCEAN ASSAULT." The back seat of the jeep has been removed to accommodate an array of surfboards, six or seven nested one atop the other. Juice climbs behind the wheel and turns the ignition. Shirley jumps in, grabs my hand, and motions me up. There is only one seat for us. I sit as far to the edge as my size allows. I try to create as much space as possible so that Shirley will have room. But there are only a few inches of vinyl remaining, and Shirley is forced into a half-crouch on the floor. Then she swings one tanned leg over mine and straddles my thigh. Her dress rides up to her hips. Out of the corner of my eye, I see that Juice's square jaw has tightened. He says nothing and stares straight ahead.

As we pull out of the parking lot, the knobby tires of the jeep dig into the gravel and spit rocks behind us. Juice pushes a cassette into the car stereo and punk rock wails out of the speakers. As if to protect me from the noise, Shirley rests her head against my ear. Covertly, she takes my hand again and gives it a squeeze. Then she lets it go.

From Sunset Beach down to San Onofre is a long way, over an hour even at high speed. The trip seems longer with icy night air rushing in your face and guitar-crazed Sex Pistols music blaring in your ears. Yet I am not uncomfortable as we make our cold, noisy way down the freeway. Above me is a blue-black sky with piercing stars. On my lap, with warm legs clasped around my thigh, with her hair tickling my face, is my first date in months. I lean back and close my eyes.

"Drum Man! Drum Man, look!" Shirley is shaking my knee and pointing at the sky, where a squadron of ten helicopters flies in formation above the San Clemente cliffs. On the tail of each copter is a yellow light flashing intermittently. Three flashes, a pause, and three more. Three-fourths time, it seems . . .

I have to press my lips close to Shirley's ear so she'll hear. "They're flying low. It's a night reconnaissance mission," I say. "Night reconnaissance."

"Mmm," says Shirley.

Juice pulls off the freeway. We drive along the service road, winding past abandoned kiosks and rolls of barbed wire. After a small parking lot, the road narrows and I see a white marker with a sign: TRAIL 1. Juice doesn't stop. Instead he accelerates and we rush past five more signs numbered 2 through 6 consecutively, and then come to a dead end. The jeep screeches to a stop. We are at the base of a hill. Halfway up is a chain-link fence with a dense row of bushes in front of it. Another sign is welded to a post:

DANGER NO ENTRY
UNITED STATES MARINE CORPS
AUTHORIZED PERSON ONLY

Shirley puts a hand on top of the windshield and lifts herself off my leg. The spot where she was sitting feels hot, then instantly cold. Suddenly Shirley is thrown back into my lap as Juice downshifts, guns the jeep off the asphalt, up the hill, and directly toward the fence. Shirley gasps. The engine roars. "DUCK AND COVER!" yells Juice.

We careen into the brush. Branches rake at the side of the jeep and scratch the top of my head. Shirley screams. But we don't become entangled in chain-link mesh—miraculously, we are on the other side of it in an open field. I twist back to see a neat rectangular opening in the fence, formerly camouflaged by brush. Now the entrance is blatant and mocking, guarded only by a few falling leaves. I glance over at Juice. A smile flickers across his lips, then disappears.

"How did you know the fence was cut there?" I ask.

For the first time, Juice speaks to me. "The surf can't be confined," he says, as if this is an axiom and I'd argued otherwise. Then he is silent again. We drive for a few more minutes, over sea grass, sage brush, and gopher holes. We drive as far as possible—to the end of a cliff overlooking the ocean, where even the omnipotent Juice decides to stop. He parks the jeep in front of a white marker with a single painted number: 9

"Where are we?" asks Shirley.

Juice waits before answering. He jumps out of the jeep, pulls a new bar of surf wax from his pocket, rips it open, and begins rubbing the wax onto a surfboard. "This is the jungle trail," he says.

There is no time for additional questions. Holding his surfboard under one arm, Juice grabs his wetsuit and starts down the trail. From the bottom of the board, the skeg protrudes—thin, curved, and dangerous, like a wasp's stinger.

I climb down the path, holding onto rocks and trees for balance. Shirley is behind me. Her breaths are high-pitched. I hear her slip in the loose dirt and she lets out a soft grunt. Branches snap back as Juice barges ahead in front of me. I hold up my arms so the plants don't whip in my face. Then I stretch the branches forward so Shirley can pass, unscathed.

The sun is just beginning to rise. The air is fresh. From a distance, the shrill call of a gull alerts its brethren that we are approaching. Soon we are down on the beach. Over the dunes, there is a reddish haze. The sand is not completely firm. Each footstep sinks in about an inch, and we leave ghostly steps behind us. I reach down to take some sand in my hand, to feel its dampness. To the south, the ocean water is dark and the beach is wide and deserted. But when I turn north, I catch my breath at the sight of the mammoth, girdered structure. It is an immense half-sphere—one hundred stories tall, with vast pipes and tubes and tanks attached. The perimeter is lit by rows of blinking lights like landing beacons of an intergalactic vessel. It is the San Onofre Nuclear Generating Station. From deep inside, it emits a low, throbbing sound.

"I'm going in," says Juice. He peels off his shirt and his trousers, unconcerned about exposing his naked buttocks as he steps into the wetsuit, and tugs it on one leg at a time. He pulls the suit over his muscular shoulders, slides his arms through the sleeves, and walks backward toward Shirley. "Zip me," he says. And she obeys.

Far past the shoreline, almost a quarter mile away, I can make out a line of breaking surf. I hear the roar of the waves. Juice heads for the water. He splashes around, rubbing cold water in his hair. Then he lies stomach down on his board, lifts his shins and feet in the air, and paddles forward with long steady strokes.

Shirley flops down in the sand and kicks off her sandals. "Drum Man," she calls out. I take one step toward her and stop.

"Is that your real name, *Drum Man*?" she asks. "It doesn't sound like a name, more of a nick—"

"Alfred," I interrupt.

"What?"

"*Alfred.* That's my real name."

"Oh." Shirley tilts her head and smiles at me. "Where are you from, Alfred?"

"New Orleans. I moved here with my Mom when I was a kid."

Shirley glances out at the water. Juice's body is a dim outline against the early morning light. "Do they have beaches in New Orleans?"

My left foot is starting to sink into the sand. I pull it out and step to the side. "Most people go to the lake. Pontchartain. There really isn't much of a beach in the city."

"You're just afraid of sharks," Shirley giggles.

"It's not that. There actually are sharks in Pontchartain. Bull sharks. Bite your butt . . . "

Shirley's hand strokes the side of her neck and rests over her chest. She gazes up at me. "Just your butt?"

"Maybe a couple other things. Depends on what looks good."

"It's romantic at the beach this early, don't you think, Alfred? Come sit by me." She pats the sand next to her invitingly. "Come sit down. I'm cold."

I don't answer, but push my drum sticks deeper into my pocket. Then, one knee at a time, slowly so as not to make a thud, I sit in the sand. Something dark—a bird or a bat—flaps its way toward the hills behind us. It circles and dives out of sight. Juice is far out near the breakers now. He is shouting. Perhaps he is singing. Shirley ignores him.

"I'm glad you're here, Alfred." She picks up a little sand and sprinkles it on my arm. I take some sand and sprinkle it back on her hand. "Don't," she coos, and waits with her hand extended until I sprinkle some more.

Suddenly a loud buzzing sound cuts through the misty dawn. It is a hateful noise like a fire alarm, and it comes from the power plant. On top of the enormous dome-shaped tank, a red beacon is flashing. The light emerges from a cylindrical nodule which looks like a concrete nipple. "May be a rupture," I muse. "Now we're toast."

Shirley laughs. "No. That just means they're ventilating chamber one."

"Quite an authority, aren't you?"

"Juice taught me."

"Oh."

Juice has caught a wave. He streams down the face, trailing one hand behind him. Soon the breakwater engulfs him, flowing over his head and around him like a soft, foamy blanket. I swallow hard and realize I've been holding my breath.

"Let's play tic-tac-toe," says Shirley. She leans on one elbow and begins to draw the lines of the game grid in the sand. "You go first, Alfred. You're *X*'s. I'm *O*'s."

With my index finger, I etch in a wobbly *X* in the center of the grid. Then, in turn, I put two more *X's* in the corners, and I've won.

"Cat's game!" says Shirley. She laughs and with quick scratches of her fingernails, like extended claws of a feline, she destroys the board. "Let's play another," she says.

Out in the water, Juice is screaming again. These are not joyous shouts of adulation for the sea. These are harsh, frantic cries. I jump up and run down the beach toward Juice. Visions of a great white shark—double-rowed fangs, bloody gums, pulsing throat, ridged gullet . . . But Juice is not flailing in the water. He has no severed limbs. He is lying atop his surfboard, chest propped up, hands gripping the side-rails of the board. His face is turned downward and he seems to be screaming directly at the sea, bellowing into its depths.

Shirley runs up beside me. "What's he doing?" I ask her. But she says nothing.

Juice begins to move. His surfboard is drawn toward us rapidly, as if carried by a strong current. He holds tight to the sides of his board, and it soon becomes clear that no current would tug him this fast through the ocean's intersecting swells. Then—and I blink—Juice's board is lifted a foot or so above the water, and there is something underneath him. It is big, about twelve feet wide, fifty feet long, covered with clots of greenish slimed sea weed. It is a large ribbed form, and it swims steadily. I start to shout, to yell, but then close my mouth when no sound comes out.

Shirley has grasped my arm. Her fingernails dig into

the flesh of my biceps and she is shivering. "Drum Man!" Her voice is a shaky whisper. "Drum Man, my god, what—"

Juice has stopped screaming. He is straddling the board now. His knees are buried in a mass of seaweed on the back of the creature—or is it a creature? A low clanking noise comes from the water. There is a slight whir, as from an engine. My legs are numb, but I manage a step forward. Then another.

The thing is closer now, and its oblong form is clear. It is a craft of some sort, a ship or a submarine. The noise it makes is loud, churring, offset by heavy metal clanks. Juice's head jerks from side to side. For a moment, I wonder if he is going to make a jump for the water. But then a line of lights flashes on at the front of the vessel. They are bright, searing—more intense than halogen—and they cut through the layers of dangling seaweed like lasers.

Shirley has wrapped an arm around my shoulders and pressed her body against me, as if the craft might somehow tow her into the water and I am an anchor. She is shaking, trembling. The ship is heading directly toward the beach. It doesn't slow down. It gives no indication of turning back to the sea. It is moving directly toward us. The craft has a new motion now, not smooth like before, but a jerking and bobbing propulsion, accompanied by grinding noises. Juice has begun to slide off to one side, and again he seems to be deciding whether or not to allow himself to fall back into the ocean, or stay on top and ride the thing in.

More of the ship is exposed above the water. It is dull gray with a graduated, pointed front like the wedged head of a prehistoric fish. On the sides are a series of angled pipes, grill-like barbs from which dangle more seaweed. The back of the ship houses two round pods, one on each side. A thin spray of steam emerges from the tail, as from a blowhole.

For some reason I am not surprised when the craft crawls up the sand on a complicated system of treads. Perhaps I would not have been surprised if the thing had sprouted wings and zoomed into the morning sky. My gaze is drawn to the triangular three-hubbed wheel sets holding the treads in place. Fins protrude from each axle. I glance up at Juice. His eyes are wide. His mouth hangs open and the tendons bulge at the base of his neck.

A motorized hatch opens on top of the craft. Two doors angle up from the mid-section. As they rise, Juice slides off. He falls twelve feet down, and I can hear him exhale when he hits the sand. It is a low empty sound, as if the wind is knocked out of him. His surfboard falls next—a loud scrape of fiberglass on metal, and a final smack when the board hits the beach.

I stare into the bright diamond-shaped lights and have to shield my eyes with my hand. A head emerges from the craft. I blink, see a man's torso, arms . . . He jumps down—a tall, slender, middle-aged man with an athletic grace. He is dressed all in black, in a uniform it seems, and he wears a scarlet beret. Curiously, no insignias or badges are evident. From his belt hang a holstered pistol and an array of tools and equipment pouches. The man's face is lean, with pockmarked cheeks. His eyes betray nothing.

He stares at me for a moment and then gazes at Shirley. Finally he speaks. "Bohemians," he says, and there is a trace of an accent which I can't quite make out. But there is something else in his tone as well, a lilting sarcasm. "Communists . . . " he says.

Another similarly dressed man, with white hair tucked under his beret, is now jumping down from the hatch. "There are no more communists." He has a similar accent but a softer voice. "Soviet Union is dead."

"Anarchists," says the tall man. "Anarchists sabotaging the power plant." He lets out a dry laugh.

From the far side of the craft comes a scuffling noise, and Juice runs out to stare at us. In his wetsuit, with seaweed dangling from his shoulders and hair, he appears even odder than the two uniformed men. He takes a step forward, a step back, and finally one more step ahead. Then he begins to shout, a swaggering chest-puffing bar-room shout. "WHAT IS THIS SHIT ANYWAY? WHO THE HELL ARE YOU? YOU CAN'T JUST—"

Instantly the tall man has punched Juice twice in the face—lightening blows to the chin and cheek which make sharp cracking noises on contact. Juice is knocked backward with the force. He falls down in the sand, unconscious—which is surprising, as Juice is big-boned and wide-shouldered and looks like he could have taken a punch. A line of blood runs from Juice's nose.

Shirley makes a low wheezing sound. I'm not sure if it's a breath or a sob. I feel the entire length of her body tense. The white-haired man steps forward. "Take it easy," he says. My chest constricts. My heart beats.

Now Shirley is yelling. She has stepped forward, thrust out her face and her bosom, and she is wiggling her chin, screeching, "YOU BASTARDS! WHO ARE YOU? YOU THINK YOU—"

Instantly she is silent. The tall man has glided behind her, twisted one arm behind her back, slid his leg around hers so she can't kick, and clamped his right hand over her mouth. The hand is clamped hard and fingers gouge into Shirley's cheeks. Her eyes bulge. She works her jaw as if trying to bite the man, but his hand stays firm—it is protected in a thick, flesh-colored rubber glove. "I told you we would catch some," he says. Then he reaches around with his left hand and rips down the side of Shirley's dress, exposing a full round breast which bounces slightly and glows in the early morning light.

I'm not normally an aggressive person. I never push in shopping lines or cut in front of others in the parking lot. Yet I pride myself on a certain inner strength, and in that instant I decide to use it, along with the only weapon that I have access to. Slowly I reach down to my side pocket and slip out one of my drum sticks. Then I grit my teeth and dash forward, conscious of my own heavy steps in the sand, aware of the way my feet sink into its dampness and have little traction. I hold the stick in front of me and I rush at the tall man. The pointed drum stick is my spear. I am the Drum Man, and a steely burst of adrenaline drives me ahead.

Of course, I am not successful. The sinewy biceps and forearm of the white-haired man clasp around my throat. My cheeks burn. Immediately, I realize the futility—in fact the comedy—of my attempt. Yet I am not ashamed. I am exhilarated, really. In my proud defeat, I gaze at Shirley's breast.

The white-haired man grabs the drum stick from my hand and breaks it in half against his thigh. He tosses it backwards over his shoulder. "Nice try, Orson," he says. He moves closer, squeezes his arm tighter, and I can feel his starched collar against the back of my head.

I manage to speak, gurgling a bit from the pressure around my throat. "Are you Marine Corps personnel?" I cough and try again. "Are you, plant security?"

The tall man looks at me, lips set, brows creased in an expression which manages to combine condescension and intolerance. It is a look reserved for annoying retarded persons dripping jello from their chins; or stuttering toll booth attendants who must be dealt with. "We, don't, exist," says the tall man in four monosyllables. "Officially . . . " His right hand has begun massaging Shirley's abdomen and moves up toward her chest. He pauses a moment, turns to look at Shirley and gaze at her soft neck. Then in a sudden motion he rips down the other side of her dress and she stands there exposed, a fertile captive maiden. Her face is flushed, and her eyes stare vacantly ahead, gray and luminous.

The next few seconds are quick, jagged, surreal. With a single motion, the tall man thrusts Shirley forward, pulls a short knife from his belt pouch, and slices open the back of her dress. She inhales sharply and the dress falls from her body. But the blade has not broken her skin. She stands perfectly still, nude as the day she was born.

The tall man begins to unbuckle his belt.

I wrench my shoulders, twist my torso, try to break free—like a bull in the chute. The grip around my neck tightens, bruises, until I can't breathe. The blood rushes in my ears and I hear my captor speaking to his comrade. "Don't. You can't!" he says loudly.

The tall man doesn't stop. He has pulled Shirley toward him. For a moment she jerks her head, writhes. But then she relaxes. Her shoulders drop, her head reclines.

The white-haired man is shouting now. "TWELVE-C!" he yells. "TRACEABLE INTERFERENCE PRO-

HIBITED!"

The tall man freezes. He is motionless like a statue posed against the outline of the sea—a slender figure holding a nude woman in front of him, fingers digging into the soft flesh of her arms. He is silent. Then he turns his head to gaze at me, to stare through me it seems—to stare at the beach behind me, and the bluff behind it, and the miles and miles of earth and trees and country beyond that. His eyes glaze over for a moment as if he is looking at nothing at all. Finally he speaks. At first, the words seem nonsensical. "Take off his clothes," he says quietly. "Take off his clothes," he says again. "*He'll* do it . . . "

My stomach tightens, twists, and my legs are unsteady. I expect the white-haired man to protest. Oddly, I expect him to protect me. I anticipate divine intervention, deus-ex-machina escape. I envision a laughing host popping out from behind a rock to tell me that it's all just a gag, and point to a hidden camera. But none of these things occur. There is no escape, and the white-haired man tugs at my shirt.

I know that I wrench again and try to free myself. I know that my arm is expertly tucked behind my back so that rays of pain shoot into my shoulder. I know that the remainder of my clothes and shoes are removed. I know that I am ashamed of my nakedness, of the image of my body in Shirley's limpid eyes. I know that I am intrigued that her eyes remain only on my upper body and seem unconcerned about the size or appearance of my genitals—and I know that I am pushed and pressed against her, that her cold breasts touch my skin, that I am forced down into the sand and Shirley is shoved on top of me.

The tall man grabs a handful of Shirley's hair and he is bending over, pushing Shirley's face down into mine, screaming in her ear. "KISS IT!" he shouts, and a drop of his hot saliva lands on my forehead. "KISS IT!" he shouts again. And I know that I am crying. Hot stinging tears of humiliation run from the corners of my eyes down the side of my face.

Then Shirley is whispering. Her soft lips touch the side of my face and she is whispering. Her eyelashes flicker on my forehead and she is whispering, humming, singing to me. She caresses my shoulders and moves her hips against mine. From somewhere above, I hear a caustic chuckle. I don't look up. I don't turn my head. I stare straight up past Shirley's blonde hair, which lies around my neck. I gaze into the crystal blue of the sky. Shirley's breaths are faster now. She is moving against me. Her body gently undulates. She slides downward, centers her pelvis upon me, and I close my eyes. In the distance, the roar of surf plays like an ovation.

The laughter above me has stopped. I open one eye and see the two men climbing back aboard their craft. Against the brightness of the sky, their black uniforms are a blur.

The men descend into the ship. They do not hesitate. They do not look back. They are creatures of the depths, and they are returning.

The hatch doors close. A droning electric noise comes from within the metal shell. Then the engine starts and the steel treads grind into the sand. When the craft enters the water, there is a long hiss like a scalding red iron under a faucet, followed by bubbling noises as the frame submerges. Finally, there is only the sound of the waves and the ecstatic cry of a distant gull.

Out of my peripheral vision, I see Juice's curled body lying fifteen feet away. But Shirley doesn't remove herself from me. She continues her insistent motions, rising and falling like the waves. And soon I am conscious of her determination, her primeval urge. I am not sure how long it takes—five minutes, fifteen, fifty. I allow her to set her own pace, and watch her arch above me. When I do look into Shirley's face, I see that although her eyelids are open, her pupils have rolled up into her brows so that only the white sclera of the eyes is visible—opaque, with tiny red veins running through it.

A few moments later, with a series of tremors and a piercing grasp of my shoulders, Shirley is finished, sated, and she collapses on top of me. In a gesture whose origin I am uncertain of, be it generosity or gratitude or fright, I have allowed Shirley to find her satisfaction, to fulfill her excitement with no thought of my own. So when she begins to remove herself from me, I gently clasp my hands over her hips and press her back down. But at that moment as I gaze into her face, her eyes swivel back into place and they stare at me without recognition. Her look is searching, perplexed, confused—and I release my grasp.

Shirley is up then. She gathers her slashed dress, ties it about her, and scampers over to Juice. I hear her talking to him. As I put on my clothes, I see Shirley rubbing Juice's chest. When I am dressed, I walk over to them. Juice has awakened. The left side of his jaw is swollen and purplish.

"Hi," I say. "Are you all right?" But neither Shirley nor Juice looks at me. "Listen, are you okay?" I ask again.

But there is no response.

Out in the water, long strands of seaweed coat the surface of the ocean. Gulls skim the swells, touch the water just barely, and return to the sky. I turn around and walk back toward the bluffs. The sun is hot now. It burns my face and forces my glance down to the sand as I walk. After a few paces, I pause and bend to pick up what was mine—one half of the broken *Dolce Ducto* drum stick. Its end is jagged and splintered.

I turn around for a final glance at the silvery ocean waves, the glimmering crests, the silhouette of Shirley bent over Juice. She is kissing him passionately—or perhaps providing mouth-to-mouth resuscitation. Near the waterline, the tread marks of the craft, wide striated indentations, have almost disappeared.

I head back toward the trail and my left foot contacts something in the sand. I bend and dig a few inches down—it is a shell, a big white seashell with a pinkish translucent interior. With two hands, I work all the caked sand out of the shell and knock it gently against my knee to clear the rest. Then I place it against my ear. I am greeted by the rushing, flowing sounds of the sea—only air movement in the aural cavity, I know, but authentic nonetheless.

I press the shell close and listen again. There is a new sound now. It is high-pitched, but reedy. It is melodic and demure like a woman's murmur, a mermaid's laughter. The sound becomes louder, more nasal. I pull the shell back an inch, feel the indentations its sharp edges have made in the skin of my cheek and in the space below my earlobe. But the laughing continues. It is incessant. I pull the shell away from my head entirely. Arms outstretched, I hold the shell in front of me as I walk back through the sand. But still I hear the sound. Its vibrations ring in my ears. So I take my broken drum stick and strike it hard—quickly and rhythmically—against the spine of the shell. *Tap, Tappa-Tap, Tappa-Tap*. And the laughter stops.

I am the Drum Man.

THE COOL SHALLOWS

An alligator is supposed to swim away from a human being. According to the Florida Department of Fish and Game, that is the characteristic of the *habitat gator*, a creature which is in its natural environment and has not suffered interference from man or chemical. The department also designates two other categories of alligators. There is the *nuisance gator*, a creature which does *not* swim away in the presence of a human being. Such a gator may have been fed, on a regular basis, by humans who were unaware that it will never make any distinction between the humans who are feeding it, and the possibility that the humans themselves are food. For an alligator, the act of eating is not an aesthetic event, a time of savoring and nibbling; feeding is a bloodthirsty impulse of gnawing and chomping and thrashing. It is a singular enterprise with a singular goal—swallowing food. According to the Darwinian chain, some gators are more successful at feeding than others. But fewer than 1 in 2,000 Florida alligators ever reaches the size of the Department of Fish and Game's third category, the *gigantus*. This is a creature, at least fifteen feet long, which must be removed immediately from all public waterways.

When Bill Pomack retired and bought a house on Lake Swenson in Central Florida, he was aware of the characteristics of alligators. He had fished with his father in Lake Okeechobee and drunk many Budweisers at Warner's Fish & Bait store, where there were three favorite topics of conversation: the foolishness of tourists, the appropriate fruit analogy for various shapes of women's breasts, and the behavior of alligators since they were put on the endangered species list in 1974 and could no longer be shot.

Bill had heard the tales of alligators that attack humans in the water: "They drag you down, try to drown you in one of their mud holes before they eat you—swallow you whole—just like that picture on the *etta-net* . . . That old golfer, Al Somebody, that got ate. They had to cut open a seventeen-foot gator's belly and see Al in there. His face was all bloated, and his hand was swelled up like an udder." This information had been recently revealed to Bill after church, by his friend Cyrus Marvin, who did not live on a lake. Cyrus lived in a mobile home park, conveniently located across the street from Wal-Mart.

When "snowbirds," winter residents, would ask him what to do in the event of an alligator attack, Bill had the answer all ready. He would tell them, "Rub the gator's belly. That's his erogenous zone. That relaxes him and he goes to sleep." However, Bill knew what you really were supposed to do if an alligator had you in its jaws. You were to try to force a thumb into the scaly slit of the creature's eye—dig the thumb in deep and hard. That would make the alligator loosen its mouth and swim away. For this purpose, Bill kept the fingernail on the thumb of his right hand sharpened into a short, triangular form.

Lake Swenson had two complexions. In the winter, the water cleared and you could see the sandy bottom, the leafy duckweed swaying in the currents and the blue-green iridescence of an occasional bass. In spring and summer, billions of microscopic algae gave the water a yellowish murky cast, and it was difficult to see more than a few feet into its depths. It was on one of these algae-ridden days in April that Bill and Cyrus decided to take their first swim of the year.

Although Lake Swenson saw the regular entrée of jet skis, fishing boats, and even an occasional sea plane, swimmers were rare. The majority of the residents surrounding the lake had their own pools or held onto the mistaken notion that, in Florida, ocean swimming was safer than lake swimming, when in fact the opposite was true. Florida averaged seven non-fatal shark attacks on humans per month and sixteen injuries from sting-rays and jelly fish. Statistics concerning alligator attacks were not available. The Department of Fish and Game only kept records about the salvage of alligators, county by county, which was actually a documentation of the number of gators that were hunted by state-licensed *Gator Boys*, who received no payment for their services, but were allowed to skin the alligators and make use of any parts of the creatures that were financially viable—or edible. Skins were sold for handbags, belts, and shoes; claws and feet were sold for key chains, lighters, and mementos; heads were sold for wall plaques and desk ornaments; intestines were sold to a chemical factory in Tallahassee which was said to derive from them a secret ingredient for vaginal ointment; livers and hearts were sold to pet food conglomerates; and tail muscle or—if time allowed—abdominal muscle was carved out and frozen into pork chop-sized alligator "steaks." A nine-foot alligator yielded approximately $1300 dollars in parts, minus the cost of shipping and waste disposal.

On the day that Bill and Cyrus decided to take their first swim, both of them had purchased new swimming trunks on sale at Kmart. They had both chosen an alligator-print pattern, although Cyrus' trunks had a pinkish hue—the only color available in size XXL. Bill's trunks were a neon green color and had plastic ridges to simulate the crenellated surface of an alligator's body.

Bill's dock had fallen into a state of disrepair and its stairs were no longer trustworthy, so entrance to Lake Swenson was in true "Indian style," as Cyrus termed it—squishing through a residue of mud and duck excrement, tramping through the torpedo grass, and finally emerging in "blue water," relatively free of objectionable elements, save for the occasional sharp edge of a freshwater clam shell. However, none of this prevented either Cyrus or Bill from carrying a can of Budweiser into the water. They held the beers above their heads to prevent water droplets from entering the open mouths of the cans (the sewage treatment plant had created an unfortunate problem in Lake Swenson in 1979 that residents had never entirely forgotten).

Given that they were drinking beer, Cyrus and Bill did not have the intention of swimming in the full-fledged sense. Their plan, though not fully verbalized, was to wade and possibly to dunk, over a period of twenty minutes, while sausage and onions cooked at low heat on the barbecue behind Bill's house. Cyrus had learned the secret to cooking an onion on a grill: "Put it on till she's black, peel the skin, and eat her . . . " Bill knew the best technique for cooking sausages: "Heat 'em low and let the juices swell, then watch for a ridge and a mushroom tip at each end . . . "

Cyrus heard an odd noise. He turned and saw Bill waving his hands and puffing out the left side of his mouth, making a "pah-pah-pah-pah-pah" sound.

"What in hell are you doing, Bill?"

"That's what the big bad-ass bass do in the water. They swim like this—" He wagged his palms. "And they open their mouths and close them again to try to catch plankton."

The conversation turned to fishing, and it was decided that it might be possible for a person to catch a fish in a lake with his bare hands. "You'd have to be real fast and have sharp fingernails," Cyrus surmised, "but you could do it. That's how the Indians did it."

"Go try it," said Bill. "I'll hold your beer."

Cyrus' beer can was empty, so he accepted the offer. "Watch this," he said, and headed toward the reedy grass and cattails just north of Bill's house. He crouched down into the water until only his head was visible. Swirling motions of water soon formed around Cyrus' shoulders as he worked his hands back and forth under the surface, pressing his fingers into the tall grass, thrusting his arms forward, trying to catch a fish.

Then Bill heard it—a throaty croaking sound, a sharp splash—and he reeled around to see a large gray form, wings outstretched, emerge from the weeds. It was a great blue heron. The bird must have been disturbed by Cyrus' fish-hunt and now it flapped past Bill. He could see the breadth of its wingspan, the directional feathers at the tips, and the long yellowish beak. Again he heard the primeval croaking of the bird. Each croak corresponded with a swelling of its neck. The bird took no notice of Bill. It circled once and landed on the dock with a final flap and of its wings and a shake of its beak. The line of feathers atop of the bird's head swept forward, the plumage fully erect for a moment before settling back into a sleek crest.

From his position in the water, Bill had a good view of the bird's claws. For a moment, he was concerned about the way these claws gouged into the wood of his dock, and he thought that the gouges might be damaging. But then he realized the foolishness of this, given that he could certainly never prevent the problem, and the dock was in such a dilapidated condition that any further damage didn't really matter. Bill was surveying his old dock when suddenly the heron lunged forward, its beak like a spear, and jabbed fiercely in Bill's direction. There was a sharp cracking noise as the tip of the beak made contact with the dock—and with a small lizard that had haplessly decided to take in some sun. The lizard writhed and squirmed, firmly caught in the sharp slender beak. Its tail whipped and its feet wiggled frantically until, with a sudden gulp, the heron swallowed the lizard whole and its body became a bulge descending down the bird's snakelike neck.

Bill was quiet for a moment. He lifted a hand to feel his own throat, which had become somewhat sunburned in the afternoon glare. "I'm hungry," said Bill. "Cyrus, are you hungry? Do you need to piss? Don't piss in my lake. You'll poison the fish."

Cyrus didn't look amused, so Bill softened his tone. "Hey, let's get more beer up at the house."

They walked out of the lake and Bill was conscious of how cool and soothing the water felt around his middle, how it massaged and relaxed him. He wanted simply to lean back in the shallows and submerge, to close his eyes and lurk under the water. He wanted to lie there and wait for food . . .

Cyrus did not find the water as appealing. He was slapping at a fly buzzing incessantly around his neck. The fly was not deterred by Cyrus' swats, nor his cursing. "Damn bugs," said Cyrus. "Do you have any repellent?"

"It's in the refrigerator," said Bill.

They trudged up the muddy beach toward Bill's back yard—"EHHHHHH!" Bill screeched. He was pointing at the barbecue. Cyrus blinked and became somewhat disoriented at what he saw—the connected links of sausages were moving off the grill, extended at a taut angle from the top of the grill to the grass—tugged by what Cyrus soon realized was a small alligator, about three feet long, which must have been attracted to the piquant aroma of grilled pork, and successfully snagged it from the grill. Bill wondered if the hot sausages might have singed the creature's mouth, but then he surmised that an alligator's gums and tongue have few nerve endings in them—how else could a gator chomp on needle-sharp fish bones?

Bill didn't have any more time to reflect about the

alligator. His right arm twitched. "Shit!" said Bill. As best as he could, he made a dash toward the grill. His bare feet dug into the muck of the beach. Cyrus began running as well, although he stayed behind Bill. When Bill headed directly for the gator, Cyrus ran to the opposite side of the grill. The alligator sensed the approach and released its sausage strand. It tried to scurry away, its body wriggling, tail swinging side to side—but it ended up moving precisely in the direction of Cyrus. There was a quick moment, a flash of a second when the gator seemed to realize this and was motionless, as if confused about which way to proceed—before it reeled to the left and tried to head toward the water.

Cyrus had no time to react to what happened next. He was astounded—dazed, really—when Bill dove onto the ground, hands outstretched, and pinned the alligator to the dirt. The gator's jaws were snapping and it made a hissing sound. Quickly, Bill pulled his left hand away from the jaws and lodged the hand just behind the alligator's head, pressing down hard, pushing two rows of sharp teeth into the dirt. Cyrus moved closer. He saw Bill's thick palm pressing down around the gator's neck. Bill's fingers were pulled back, fingernails digging into the ground to avoid the teeth.

"GOT 'EM!" Bill said triumphantly. His breathing was heavy. He looked up and smiled.

"I got 'em," he said again. But then his smile faded.

He blinked, twisted his head, as if unsure what to do next.

"You're like that crocodile guy in the movies," said Cyrus. "That Australian guy, the one who creeps around and has a knife and a girl that helps him . . . " His voice trailed off, as he was struck for a moment by just how *unlike* the famed wilderness star Bill appeared—with his flabby pink torso, his pudgy hands, his psychedelic green shorts. And the alligator was so small. It had ceased to squirm, and seemed to have either accepted defeat or was attempting a new tactic of escape—feigning exhaustion or mortal injury and waiting for the crucial moment when, in an adrenaline-filled burst, it would dash and flee to freedom. But that moment was long in coming . . .

For several minutes Bill squatted, chest heaving, clenching the gator. He seemed content to do just that, as if the joy of the capture was a moment to be savored and extended. However, soon Bill himself began to squirm, to roll his neck from side to side and twist his torso. Cyrus realized that Bill's position—one knee in the dirt, one knee up, spine bent forward and hands pressed down—must be quite uncomfortable. "What are you gonna do with it, Bill?" he asked.

"Huh?"

"Watcha gonna do with the gator?"

Bill laughed, and it sounded more like a cackle. "I'm gonna eat it!" Bill's eyes had a reddish gleam.

"Naw, he's too small," said Cyrus, "He's just a baby.

Not even any tail meat."

"I know," said Bill. But his forehead creased and he looked a bit uncertain. Then his face cracked into a grin. He began to nod his head. The nodding became more rapid, rhythmic. "I'm gonna rub his belly," said Bill.

Cyrus didn't have time to consider this, or to protest, because Bill had worked his right hand around the gator's abdomen, and his left hand behind its front legs. With a quick surge of motion—an uplift, swivel, and shoulder roll—Bill managed to turn the gator on its back. Its tail whipped back and forth and its claws wriggled at the air. Its head, oddly, seemed to be lunging backward into the dirt. Bill moved one knee forward until he clamped it on top of the gator's tail. He centered his left palm on the gator's chest, and the veins bulged on top of his hand as he pressed down on the whitish underbelly.

"Watcha gonna do to it?" Cyrus asked again.

"I told you . . . " said Bill slowly. His mouth hung open. He cleared his throat and stared intently at the animal. Again, the gator seemed to be attempting a default tactic, for now it was completely motionless. It lay there, head partially buried in the sandy soil, tail trapped beneath Bill's thick knee. Even the claws were still.

Carefully, Bill loosened the grip of his right hand. He rotated his wrist, just a little at first, then paused. Keeping the pressure down, Bill extended his index finger, then his middle finger and began, gently, to stroke the alligator's abdomen.

For a moment the alligator's body relaxed. Its head arched upward, out of the dirt, and its legs drooped down a bit—but then all four sets of claws clenched and the gator rolled its head from side to side. It made a high-pitched sound, almost a mew. A rasping alligator mew . . .

Bill had developed a look of tender concentration, a look that Cyrus had never seen in him before. At that point, Bill seemed utterly unaware of his surroundings, of his posture, of Cyrus and, as if mesmerized, he stared down at the small alligator and softly caressed its belly.

Cyrus walked closer, but stayed behind the grill for protection. He wanted to see the alligator's face, and was struck by the strength of his desire to do so. He wanted to see the creature's expression. Of course, this was difficult, given that the head was half buried in dirt. But Cyrus tried anyway. He tried to see its eyes. He put one hand on the wooden sideplate of the grill to steady himself and leaned forward.

The next few moments happened in a blur—a fusion of noise, motion, and color.

An immensely loud guttural sound, an enormously amplified bellowing, came from the shrubs beside Bill's house. The noise was accompanied by snapping branches and crackling leaves, and then it seemed as if the entire row of shrubbery had come to life, whipping and swaying and releasing a thick green form—writhing, clawing—it was a huge alligator, as long as a car. In a lightning motion, the alligator clawed toward Bill—and then it was right next to him. The enormous jaws opened, revealing yellowish teeth and reddish gums—

The jaws snapped shut and bit off Bill's left foot.

Cyrus felt a jolt in his chest. He saw the blood rushing from Bill's severed ankle, turning the grass a surreal red. He saw the alligator opening its jaws again—and Cyrus reacted—he pushed hard, toppled the grill over, pushed it down on the creature's back. Red hot embers and gray ash piled on the gator, releasing circles of steam. The alligator turned its head for a moment, as if surprised, to look at Cyrus; and Cyrus gazed for a deep long second into the dark reptilian eye. He stared down into the moistness of the opening. He looked into the eye, into the mystery and power of its depth—and then the eye shut. The huge gator turned toward the water.

The baby alligator had fled a few seconds earlier. Side by side, both creatures headed for the lake. Cyrus could see the triads of ridges on their backs and the swaying of their tails, almost in unison . . . Then they were splashing into the water—heads, backs, feet—streaming through the glass-smooth surface of the lake . . . And then they were gone.

Bill was motionless. In shock. His eyes were shut. He didn't even groan as the blood gushed from a vein in his calf. Cyrus knew he couldn't waste a second. He glanced back and forth for something to tie off the leg to stop the bleeding—A rope? A cord? A handkerchief? There was nothing. Only one chance, one choice—and Cyrus tore down his swimming trunks, yanked them off his body, one leg, then the other. The trunks got stuck on his foot but he grabbed at them, felt something crack in his knee—it didn't matter. He had them off, and he was only faintly aware of the odd sensation of sunlight on his naked buttocks. He bent over and slid the elastic waist of the trunks over Bill's bloody stump of a leg. His fingers slipped in the blood, but it didn't matter. He found the waistband and cinched it with all his might until the cord dug deep into the skin below Bill's knee. Then Cyrus pressed one palm down to hold the cord in place and looped it around again, pulled as hard as he could and repeated the process—a triple-wound tourniquet. He tied it off with a square knot.

Cyrus hoped he was successful. He had to be successful. And fortunately, it seemed as if the blood flow had subsided. He could see caked red dirt between the grass blades, where before there had been a scarlet pool.

Cyrus looked around—maybe they could reattach Bill's foot? Micro-surgery, laser surgery, plastic surgery, right? He glanced to his left, to his right, behind him even—craning his neck. But the foot was gone. Devoured. It was inside the alligator. It went down the gator's throat and into its abdominal cavity where hydrochloric acid and enzymes would eat away at the foot, make it swell to three times its normal size, and then dissolve it into a pulpy mass.

Cyrus closed his eyes and screamed. "HELP!" And he realized that it was the first time during the ordeal that either of them had shouted. "HELLLLLLP!" he screamed again. It felt good to shout. Important. Necessary. "Call for HEEEELLLLLLLLP!"

It wasn't long before Bill's neighbor appeared, an old woman in a leopard-print polyester robe—she took one look at Cyrus' naked body crouched over Bill, and she started to run back to her house. "HELP!" Cyrus yelled again. "He's hurt!" The woman stopped, turned, took another look—and started running again.

But it really was only a few minutes more. An ambulance shrieked to the house, and the paramedics were working on Bill—with stethoscopes, hypodermic needles, bandages, and medical tape. The medics only glanced for a moment at Cyrus' nudity.

One of the paramedics was pacing the yard, eyes to the ground. Finally his gaze turned to Cyrus, who had moved over to a tree and, with two hands, was trying to cover his genitals. "Where's the foot?" the paramedic asked.

Cyrus shook his head slowly. "Alligator . . . " he said.

The paramedic stood perfectly still for a moment. His eyes widened. But there was no further discussion. Then Bill was in the emergency van, and the siren was on.

They wouldn't let Cyrus ride in the van.

Following the attack, three separate Gator Boys were employed to find the gigantus in Lake Swenson. They used airboats and sonar and gator bait, severed boar carcasses. They came early in the morning, at dusk, and at midnight. But the big alligator was never found.

Bill had six weeks of bed rest, ten months of physical therapy, and then he was given a metal foot and a plastic one. The artificial feet attached to a square titanium post on the stump of his leg. They clicked on and off. Bill could walk on the metal foot, but he had a definite limp and had to move slowly. He could wear the plastic foot for swimming, but he refused to swim for two years, even in pools. He stayed away from water for a long while, but then developed a sudden passion for it. He bought a snorkel, a dive knife, and a CO_2-powered harpoon gun. He bought some swim fins with a molded cushioned insert to fit around his prosthetic foot.

Frequently, you can spot his rippling wake or bobbing snorkel in Lake Swenson—near the shore, or sometimes in the reeds. If you go closer, you can see his air bubbles and mud-covered body. And if you sit next to him at church, you can smell the odor of the lake.

ALIEN IN BLISS

Tokyo, Japan – 1989

I only had 800 yen left. I'd just spent the last of my emergency money on a room in Sanjo Ryokan, a dilapidated old boarding house near the red-light district of Ikebukuro. Most likely, only foreigners on a shoe-string budget would even consider such a residence. But the front desk clerk, a beautiful Japanese girl with perfectly bobbed hair, had feigned lack of concern when I took a ten-thousand yen note out from under the insole of my shoe to pay for the room. I pretended that was the normal place to keep money. And I bowed when she gave me the key.

The Sanjo entranceway was a museum of old soy sauce wrappers and crusty house slippers. However, there were advantages to the location. The 7-Eleven (*Sebenu Erebenu*) was at the end of the block. The subway station was close. A noodle house was across the street. And when I opened the door to my room, I could see little frogs hopping joyfully outside on the window ledge. Inside the room, a row of brownish mushrooms grew along the back wall, emerging out of the tatami mat—perhaps from ancient seeds. Were the mushrooms edible? Were they my private nutrition source? Conducting a taste test seemed like a bad decision . . .

I brought in my suitcase and set my Casio electric keyboard case on top of it. The room needed a musical initiation. So I unzipped the case and switched on the keyboard's power button. The indicator light glowed bright green—a good omen. The batteries still had a long life ahead of them. I began to improvise a tune. Loneliness leads to introspection. And introspection leads to poetry—perhaps tritely so . . . And poetry leads to music, at least in my case. I switched the rhythm button to Tempo 7. Soon my fingers found a melody. The lyrics came in a prescient stream:

> I don't know
> What the girls think
> Secretly
> Underneath it
>
> I foresee
> Inspiration
> Not alone—
> Conjugation

Then I decided.

The idea hit with the force of a gale wind. I could make money playing the piano! I would play and sing in the street, like Bob Dylan. The little speakers in the piano would be loud enough. I could put out a hat for tips. But I didn't have a hat . . . I could open the carrying case and tuck in a few yen as a hint. I would add a new musical ambiance to the city. I would meet people too.

It was a very good plan.

I slid the piano into its case and grabbed my skateboard. At twenty-four, I was arguably too old for a skateboarder, but now I was glad that I hadn't resisted the urge to bring the board with me to Tokyo. I tucked the last of my Japanese yen into the piano case, zipped it shut, locked the door to my room, and ran down the hallway. My steps rang heavy on the old dark wood. I headed downstairs and watched my feet so I wouldn't trip. The dawning of an idea was a dangerous time.

Outside, the sky had darkened, and the air was cold. The crescent shape of a troubadour's moon hung above. I jumped on the skateboard and kicked twice. The urethane wheels made a smooth, whirring sound on the asphalt. And frogs jumped out of my way. I dragged a toe to slow down and took a deep breath. I was a little frightened. Only a little—stage fright. What could happen? Even if I didn't make any money, the anecdotal value of skateboarding through Tokyo at night to be a street musician was an experience I couldn't deny myself.

A gust of wind chilled my spine. It would be too cold playing in the street. I could play inside the subway station. That's what musicians did in New York, right? I headed toward Ikebukuro Station, the enormous subway hub of northwest Tokyo. I made it to the entrance and descended the stairs, holding the banister and sticking close to the wall. When I got to the turnstiles, I tucked the cased piano under my arm, so it didn't look like I was toting a cased submachine gun.

For 9:00 pm, the station was a lot more crowded than I had expected. The concession stands were still open, surrounded by crowds of cigarette-buying, newspaper-clutching Japanese customers. A few people gawked at the skateboard, so I pulled it closer and glanced around, looking for the optimum place to play. An ache started in my stomach and I couldn't help feeling like a criminal, a spy planting a bomb. But I wasn't going to do any damage. Just liven up the place a little.

Finally I found a prime spot near the ticket machines in the center aisle. Everybody had to buy a ticket, right? About ten feet from the main crowd, I could lean against a support column. I sat on the skateboard, unzipped the keyboard case, and laid the instrument across my knees. A few funny stares, but no one stopped me. I switched on the power and made sure the rhythm was still set to #7. Then I cranked up the volume all the way. I would play my new song. It had a good swing beat. And suddenly it had a title: ALIEN IN BLISS.

The introduction was a rolling slap-syncopated bass line. The electronic tones resounded in the big station hall, especially the rhythm sounds—sizzling cymbals, hissing snares, throbbing kettles. A few people turned, slowed their pace in mid-stride. I sang to them in a deep, loud voice.

> Don't ask me what your mama thinks
> Abstractly about it all now
> I'm just cool, not lethargic
> Profoundly, Mister Bard-it

Two businessmen laughed, tossing their heads and clapping their hands. They watched me intently. I smiled and sang more. I had the bridge already, and I crooned it out:

> I'm just cool
> It's my business
> Hopefully
> Inconspicuous

One of the men walked over to me and spoke in halting English. "*Haro*. You are a good musician."

"Thank you."

The man stared down at the keyboard, bending over with a keen examining eye. He peered down as if trying to see between the keys. "That ees Casio machine?"

"Yes. How did you know?"

"I have Casio machine at my house."

"Really? Would you like to play this one?"

The man shuddered and stepped back. He twitched. "No sank you." Then he glanced quickly to the right and left and right once more, as if to make sure no one had witnessed the offer. So I started to sing again. My voice was warmed up now.

> Now I really understand
> What it means to be
> An older attraction
> Sitting in a tree
>
> Above board, all around
> Like aliens in bliss
> Just another normal day
> Nothing is amiss

The man crouched down. His mouth was close to my ear. "How much ees Casio machine een America?" he whispered.

I kept the music going and answered quickly. "Oh, I paid about a hundred and twenty dollars. Fifteen thousand yen."

He grunted. "This piano is very cheap in America."

"Is it more expensive in Japan?

The man`s jaw tensed, but he didn't reply.

Three more people had stopped to watch the interaction. It must be an odd sight: a nervous Japanese man in a stained suit bending over to have a secret conversation with a piano-playing foreigner, a *gai-jin*, who was sitting cross-legged on a skateboard in the middle of Ikebukuro station.

Soon four more Japanese joined the crowd. It had taken this first questioning man to start, and now my audience was growing fast. I needed to play more. That was very clear. "Hello!" I greeted the audience, shooting my voice across the floor like a televangelist:

> I don't know
> What the girls think
> Privately
> In the pinkish
>
> I'm amused
> With the toothpicks
> And in vain
> It's a privy-ledge

The crowd probably couldn't understand all the words, but it didn't matter. Music was an international language. The audience was clapping in time to the rhythm of the song. I almost forgot! I opened the piano case to reveal the small pile of Japanese money I had stuffed inside it as a hint. Someone snickered, but I kept playing. My fingers flew over the keys.

About twenty people were watching now. They were standing shoulder-to-shoulder, hip-to-hip, all clapping and smiling like it was New Years' Day. I nudged the case forward with the toe of my shoe. An older woman stepped out of the crowd. Hesitating as if she were tossing a peanut to a screeching lemur at the zoo, she dropped in a few coins.

"*Domo arigato,*" I thanked her, and kept singing without missing a beat.

Five or six more people tossed money into the case. There was a thousand-yen note! That alone was worth eight bucks. So I switched to another song which also had a snappy pop beat. The audience's clapping, a flurry of swatting palms, adjusted to the new rhythm. The crowd was getting even larger. Two teenaged boys walked by. One of them wore a cowboy hat and jeans. The boys pushed in front of the crowd and danced a few quick steps—bodies lunging, arms pumping, flashing peace signs with their index and middle fingers. After a brief moment of glory, they dashed away. Their fame was only a tiny flicker in the limelight.

Off to the left, a pretty Japanese girl in a bright red dress was staring at me. I could feel a distinct attraction, an electromagnetic force. She gazed with amazement and adoration. She didn't even blink. Humans are bundles of electric waves, fields, and sensors—the girl made my *electroreceptors* tingle . . . Her gaze alone was worth the whole evening. I smiled and made sure to sing a few lyrics just to her. She didn't smile back, but her eyes gleamed even more. They seemed to moisten. And then she knelt so our faces were at the same level.

I would have stared at her all night, but there were thirty or forty in the crowd at least now! Clapping in perfect sync. There was a magic to being a master showman—and a responsibility. I scanned the audience and made eye contact with everyone. Unfortunately, my butt hurt from sitting on the skateboard, and my left leg was going to sleep. But I couldn't stop and break the spell. I wouldn't violate the audience's pleasure. Besides, there was at least two hundred dollars' worth of yen already in the case, in fifteen minutes! This audience deserved my best performance.

I played a series of improvisations, fingers skimming over the keys in rapid bursts, left hand rolling out the bass. But now the crowd's attention was waning. Why? I played a simpler, more repetitious melody. Soon the synchronized clapping started again. The energy was building once more. *They had to be able to clap in time to the song.* Beating their hands and swaying their bodies, they could be part of the music. Or was it something else? *A group clap.* A unison. A perfect synergy of attention and participation. And I was its center—its neurological pulse.

Where was the girl in the red dress? Dammit, she had left. I was surprised at my feeling of loss. I didn't even know the girl. But the power indicator light on the keyboard was flashing. The batteries were getting low. My back hurt. My thighs ached. The crowd had swelled to fifty or sixty now. The show had to go on.

There she was! Carrying something under her arm, the girl in red ducked through the crowd. She was about twenty-nine or thirty, with red lips and a flawless complexion. She held out a wrapped gift for me. "*Pu-re-sento,*" she said shyly, and lay the box at my feet.

"*Arigatoo,*" I answered. But her expression didn't change. It was as if she hadn't even heard. "Thank you," I repeated in English, and she blushed. It was the English words she wanted.

She had a nice figure, a soft figure. Not like some so-called California beauties who exercised themselves into hard taught sinewy bodies. This was unhindered natural shapeliness, smooth curves and—

"*DA-ME!* BAD!" Two uniformed guards shouted at me. They broke through the crowd, shoving and stomping.

I stopped playing and looked up at their razor-pressed uniforms and leather accessory belts. "The music is bad?" I asked, and gave a sorrowful look. I was a poor humble prophet whose gift, sadly, had been misunderstood.

"BAD! IT IS FORBIDDEN!"

My cheeks burned. I reached to pull back the piano case. Then I caught a glimpse of the flared nostrils of one of the guards. He stared down at what was now quite a big pile of money inside the case. There were folded bills, handfuls of coins, and huge shiny five-hundred-yen pieces.

Suddenly, two handsome young Japanese men in double-breasted jackets stepped forward. "It's okayee," one said to me. The other spoke to the guard in a flurry of angry Japanese syllables. Below their perfect blow-dried hair, the young businessmen's faces were flushed. They tottered a little, too. "PLAY MORE!" the English-speaking one encouraged and gave a loud, lone clap.

I smiled. I had some supportive fans. They were protecting me from the evil authorities. So I played a few more bars and the two Japanese men stood together and clapped intently to the rhythm, clapped as if they were committed to having fun at a party even though the birthday cake was stolen and all the guests had the mumps.

But the guards stalked forward again. Two pairs of shiny black boots with thick molded soles touched the sides of my piano case. "BAD!" shouted a sweaty-faced guard again.

One of the young Japanese businessmen was laughing loudly. He made an odd snorting sound, stepped directly in front of the guard, and yelled in his face: "*FUCKU* YOU!" Then the other man giggled. It was amazing that they flaunted authority like this. They were drunk though, which in Japanese society was said to give them an extra freedom. But the men had cursed at the guards *in English.* The English words themselves gave them a special liberty, a mocking glee. Probably the men thought the guards wouldn't understand. Or maybe after years of watching American movies, they thought this was acceptable speech for Americans. This was how Americans related. It was natural! It was fun!

The guards were eyeing my money again. I grabbed the case and zipped it closed without even taking time to put back the piano. Then I slipped my skateboard and gift under one arm, piano and case under the other, and marched toward the exit with my back straight and head high. I was a proud, mistreated musician who wouldn't lose his spirit.

One of the Japanese businessmen hurried over to me. He tapped my arm and began to speak, but I wasn't listening. I had spotted the girl in the red dress. She was peeking around a pole. I walked toward her, ignoring the man completely. Maybe this was rude, but there were priorities.

The girl saw me and glanced down for a moment, but she didn't move away. "Hi," I said. She smiled and gazed down at the floor again. A blush started at the base of her neck. "What's your name?" I asked.

"*Komako desu,*" she trembled. "Ni-su to meetu you." She laughed and covered her mouth.

"Thank you for the present."

"You, are, wel-come." This time she couldn't help it. The laughter erupted before her hand could cover her lips. English-speaking was hilarious.

"You are good at English!"

"No . . . " She shook her head, almost a frisson, and waved her hand back and forth in rapid horizontal strokes.

Underneath all of this, she glowed. She swam in the compliment like a glistening little mink.

"I am thirsty," I said. "Shall we drink some coffee? *Chotto coohi . . .*" I was proud to use the buffer *chotto*. It actually meant "a little," but was used to soften a request so it wouldn't seem too forward. I hoped it was even a bit sly.

Komako hesitated and caught her breath with a tiny whimper.

I touched her shoulder. "Let's go this way." I guided her toward the stairs. But I had absolutely no idea at all where I was heading. And no idea if there were even any places open. We exited the subway and crossed the intersection. The Tokyo McDonald's was closed. The bar on the corner was dark. The *Miraku Coffee-Tea* was locked tight. I decided to say something to show how relaxed I was in the situation. "Are you thirsty?"

I thought I heard a sigh of affirmation. So we walked up *Ekimae Dori*, but all the stores were shut. A man with eyes as piercing as drill bits passed us on the sidewalk. He stared at me—a foreigner, walking so closely, so late at night, with a Japanese girl. I looked away and gently put a hand on Komako's lower back.

Back home in San Diego, a Marine Corps lieutenant who had been stationed in Tokyo told me exactly what to say if you wanted to sleep with a Japanese girl. He claimed to be an expert on the subject. You were supposed to say, "Let's drink morning tea together"—implying that the evening would be shared as well. But I couldn't say it yet.

There were no more coffee shops this far from the station, only row houses and love hotels, with rooms rented by the hour. Komako had to realize this too, or at least she could easily figure it out. We were in a residential neighborhood. There had been no stores for the past three blocks. I would just walk back to my room in Sanjo. If Komako didn't want to come in, she would say so. At this time of night, we weren't going to play checkers or mahjong. She had to know this. The Japanese don't share Western ideas of the sinfulness of sex, I reminded myself. It was a natural phenomenon to be enjoyed like anything else, in its proper place. It was considered harmful for people to go without sex. My room in Sanjo Ryokan was just down the street from a big love hotel. How much more proper could it be? I walked faster, for my health.

The Sanjo entrance way was dirtier and messier than I remembered. It was a jumble of shoes, donut wrappers, unlaced sneakers, and broken umbrellas thoughtfully left for the next travelers. I saw Komako staring at a cracked mirror. Of course, she made no comment. We took off our shoes. I decided that it was actually somewhat annoying to have to take your shoes off each time you went into a building . . .

We walked up the dim narrow stairway, and I held Komako's hand at the last step so she didn't trip over a strip of jagged wood. I unlocked my door. I was glad that in the darkness of the evening, you couldn't see the mushrooms growing against the wall. And my room was tidy—because I hadn't had time to unpack. It even seemed relatively clean. Komako would like that. And she did. Her eyes told all. She relaxed and leaned against the wall—waiting, breathing . . .

I sat down on the futon and gave the space beside me an inviting pat. Komako hesitated a moment, then sat down a few inches away. I unzipped the case and switched on the piano. Often I gave my dates a special piano lesson. The lesson included an "Improvisation Test" that I had invented. It was a duet. I would play the last four descending notes of a C-minor scale over and over like a bass line, and I would show the girl the first three notes of the scale. She could play them in any order, in any time, in any combination, and it would always sound pretty good. A little boring, but harmonically okay. With the test, I would help my date discover her hidden musical talent. I would nurture her creative ability. And I always gave a grade on the Improvisation Test. Whether the girl tapped keys timidly with false fingernails, banged two notes together in a clumsy push, or depressed keys precisely in intellectual fascination, the grade was always the same: "*A* plus plus."

But right then, right there, I didn't want to have to go through the damn test. So I played a song for Komako, a soft ballad. Then I kissed her. Just like that.

She wasn't a bad kisser. A little liquor-breathed and shy perhaps. But after a few minutes I realized that it wasn't shyness, but a deliberate effort at naivete, like a professional gambler feigning amateur status. Every once in a while I would touch her gently, and her lips would relax and press and tingle. Then she would control them again, forcing them back into clumsy pecks.

I fumbled with her dress, played with the buttons, pulled at the zipper, and after half an hour she let me undo the top. I took off my shirt and tried to unzip Komako's skirt, but she pulled my hand away. And moaned.

An hour more of this. No go.

Finally, I lay back and chuckled a little. Hemisphere to hemisphere, the game didn't really change much . . . Komako glanced at me. Her eyebrows arched. "*Nani*? What?"

I didn't answer. I put my arm gently around her waist and lay back on the futon. I closed my eyes. I relaxed my shoulders. Silently, I counted my breaths: One . . . Two . . . Three . . . Four . . . It was a sleep-inducing exercise. I rarely got to eighty without dozing off.

A little while later, I woke up when Komako lay on top of me completely naked and started kissing my neck. I took her by the shoulders and rolled her over, watching her expression of simultaneous surprise, pleasure, and submission. Then she arched her back. As I suspected, she was neither shy nor naive in bed. I remembered a line from a Japanese movie. It ran through my head like a poem. "The skin is the most beautiful part when you make love."

Komako whispered something. Her hot moist breath tickled my cheek. But I couldn't understand her. I wasn't sure if she was speaking Japanese or English. She pressed her mouth close to my ear and whispered to me again. "My firstu *orugazun*."

"Your first orgasm?"

She smiled and hid her face in the pillow.

"Well congratulations," I said, a bit surprised at her frankness. What was I supposed to say? Again, different Japanese attitudes . . . How did she know the word?

Somehow, I didn't believe her. Not that she didn't know what she was saying. But she was deliberately speaking simply, using the clearest words so I would be sure to understand. Perhaps she was saying what she thought I wanted to hear, giving me another gift . . . Or was she saying this to convince herself. I didn't know. And there were no more clues. Soon we fell asleep.

Outside the hatch window, birds were pecking and fluttering. I forced open my eyes. A spear of light pierced through the shutter.

Komako was gone!

It was 10:30 am. Maybe she just went to the bathroom? But all of her clothes were gone, too. And she had set her present conspicuously on the little table next to the futon.

No note. No parting tears. No morning tea.

I sat up. Maybe she had to work? It was Sunday, though. Could she work in a shop? A department store that was open Sundays?

Doubtful.

I picked up my gift, wrapped in pale pink tissue paper with golden bows. In Japan, the beauty of the wrapping was said to be as important as the gift itself. A nicely-wrapped, cheap present was considered much better than an unwrapped, expensive one.

Cheap or expensive, wrapped or unwrapped, it didn't make much difference to me. It was the spirit of gift-giving that mattered. Carefully, I untied the ribbon and loosened the tissue paper to reveal a silver box, a hope chest etched with *kanji,* traditional Japanese characters. I lifted the lid. Inside was an assortment of rice crackers: plain, frosted, peppered, and sea-weed covered.

Most of the crackers were broken and crumbling in their plastic tray.

REMEDY

"Get him the water," says my grandmother. She points.

I walk around the hospital bed where my grandfather lies with one leg exposed. It's a soft pulpy leg, a baby's leg, with a large plastic tube running up it and into his groin. His face and hairless scalp look infant-like as well. His jaws seem to chew some imaginary tobacco, even though he gave it up years ago.

I feel nauseous and hold onto the bottom of his bed for balance. The room grows dim. I lift the muscles of my eyebrows, force my eyes open wider, and try to bring back the light. I breathe and stare at the water glass, a pink glass with a plastic straw attachment. I take it in my hand and, with two fingers, insert the straw between my grandfather's lips.

He sucks in the water. His jaws stop their chewing for a while. Then they start again.

"Howard," says my grandmother. "What are you doing with your face? Don't do that with your face."

A red-haired nurse walks in. Her lipstick is not red, it's orange. And there are orange lipstick smudges on white shiny teeth. "How is everyone today?" She smiles. Her earlobes are sunburnt.

Over the intercom, a voice announces, "Code Blue." Then two stretchers are wheeled quickly past our room. Blue sheets cover the bodies and faces.

The nurse walks over to the bed. "We have a little medication that will make you feel super-duper," she says, and begins to hum. Her hands are covered with green latex gloves. She opens two foil wrappers, presses out disc-shaped pills, tears off the top of a plastic cup of apple juice, slides a gloved finger into my grandfather's mouth, pulls down his lower jaw, and drops in the pills. Then she pours in some juice and closes his mouth.

He doesn't choke. The juice does not go into his nasal passages. It goes down his throat. The nurse must know how to do it right. Just where to set the pills. How much juice to pour in. Where to slide in her finger. Like on a horse . . . To get in the bit, you stick your thumb in its mouth all the way in the back. Otherwise, your fingers get caught between its teeth. You can lose a thumb that way.

The medication is strong. The doctor told us that. I pick up a wrapper off the floor: Hydromorphone Hydrochloride 4mg. Brand Name: Dilaudid®. Now, my grandfather's eyes are open wide. They are glazed and a little red.

"Howard," says my grandmother, "I'm here, and so is

Robert." She pats the mattress.

He turns his head to look, only a few degrees, then stares forward again. "Where's my grandson?" he says.

"I'm right here." I walk over to the other side of the bed and rub my grandfather's arm, below the blue bruising of the intravenous.

"I feel like shit," he says. His pupils are dilated. He doesn't blink. He stretches out his chin, raises his head a half inch off the pillow, lets it fall again. "And I'm bored. I want you to sing *Raindrop*s."

"I'll sing it at Thanksgiving."

He sighs, almost moans, "Why won't you sing *Raindrops*?"

I glance at my grandmother. "Now Robert doesn't want to sing in here," she says.

"Please, Robert. Sing *Raindrops* to me . . . " There is saliva on his bottom lip. "Sing *Raindrops* to your Grandpa."

His face is pale, his lips liver-colored. He used to take me fishing, correct my casting, put the worm on the hook when I didn't want to. He used to row a boat with steady strokes. He used to pull out the hooks with his fingers. He didn't care when blood got on his pants.

My throat is dry, and I swallow. I sing the song that my sister and I sang in the car when we were little. The song that my grandfather has a cassette of us singing. My grandmother walks into the hall. I don't know all the words, but I improvise. I don't cry. Finally, I am done.

"You can sing that at my funeral," he says.

"Well, there are no funerals today." My voice is cheery. Like the nurse.

The next day, the doctor says Granpa is better. They move him into another wing. He has his own room and his own TV. He has a different kind of bed. It looks almost normal, except it can bend in half, and underneath it there is a buzzing silver machine with a brown hose. He sits upright with a channel changer in one hand, a red emergency button in the other. On the nightstand is a bowl of jelly beans.

"I feel terrible," he says. "Jesus Christ, they give me so much medicine, I don't know what I'm doing. I don't know what I'm saying."

"Yeah, the pills can be pretty strong."

"I don't even know what reality is sometimes."

"Well that's okay. Neither do I . . . " I laugh a little.

He doesn't laugh back. "How's your job?"

"It's okay. I get through the days. I might look for a better job, though."

"What's the matter with this job?" He stares at me. "This job isn't good enough for you?"

"Well, all I do is look at a computer screen . . . It hurts my eyes and gives me a headache. When I get home, I just want to drink scotch and go to bed."

"For Chrissake, a job's a job, understand? A job's a job.

A man has to earn a good living, that's all. You have to earn a good living like I did—understand?" He picks up a purple jellybean and brings it to his mouth. Then he squeezes it between his thumb and index finger and wipes the ooze on the sheet.

"So how are your girlfriends? Any good dates lately? Or aren't any of the girls good enough for you?"

"Really I'm just too busy with work and school. Once in a while I go out. But usually I don't have the time. Or the money."

"You still like girls don't you? You're not a *fag* that likes show tunes are you? Are you a FAG?"

"No, I'm not a homosexual."

"Good." He spits a half-dissolved jellybean onto the floor. "I'm going to sleep now."

I walk into the hall and smell the artificial strawberry scent of disinfectant. My nostrils burn. I hold my breath all the way down the corridor and reach the exit door without breathing. My chest aches, but I manage four more huge strides away from the building. Then I allow myself to inhale. Long gasping breaths. My hands are trembling. I tell myself to relax. I lean back my head and open my arms wide, holding them out, stretching, letting the sun permeate my body. Breathing smoothly now, I gaze into the afternoon sky.

A seagull is above, hovering over the hospital building. Its wings are outstretched—but the bird is absolutely stationary and seems a visual illusion . . . It must be caught, positioned on top of an air vent, directly over the exiting stream. I realize that our postures are as identical as bird and human can be: arms and wings extended, motionless . . .

I wonder if the bird sees me. And what it feels at this exact moment . . . I close my eyes and try to project my mind into that of the bird, into its bird brain, and radiate a deep feeling of affection, connection—a feeling of *love.* Can the bird perceive this? Does it know?

Suddenly, a loud buzzing noise comes from the top of the building—perhaps a generator has kicked in. The gull drops down a few feet, flaps its wings, and flies away.

RIDING WITH THE DOCTOR

I am an expert on folklore, and I know all about the masks with noses shaped like penises. These masks are a crucial element of rural Louisiana Mardi Gras celebrations, a folk life which we must preserve, as it is a significant heritage. I, Dr. Hoyt Leblanc, am in an enviable position, as I am both a native of the "Cajun" region of Louisiana ("Cajun" is formulated from the word "Acadien," in a unique contraction) and an accomplished Doctor of Folklore Studies. Frequently, I give lectures on various aspects of culture at the university and at the church, for the edification of the populace. I see you are staring at my mustache. Isn't it grand? It is in the "full brush" style fashioned in the late 1870s, but most popular in the early spring of 1877. I allow the side brushes of my whiskers to drop in a *demi-cercle*. All of the ladies love to touch my facial hair and feel it on their skin. They say, "Mais chère, lemme tosh dat moostache."

On Tuesday next, I am going to the Mardi Gras festival

in Duson, where I will be both spectator and participant. This is known as "multi-tracking," when one appears in a position with two separate functions, e.g., observateur / participateur, which affords a unique entrance point into the societal characteristic.

You are looking at my pocket? That's only the outline of a tube, see—Moustache Lotion. I buy it from the distributor in New Orleans. Sniff . . . Sniff the scent. It's made from the original recipe developed before *la dérangement from Nova Scoshe.* Sniff . . . That's the smell of nutria pelt oil mixed in with the gelatin base. A nutria is a large melon-shaped rodent with a pointed snout.

You assumed that I would be the capitaine of this year's Mardi Gras "course," didn't you? Actually, although many feel that I have the stamina and musculature to be leader, this year I will not command the begging for chickens. However, I am very close friends with the capitaine's brother. In fact, our masks—with beads and sticky fur on the chins—share the same noses, made from limp carrots spray-painted tan.

As my folkloristic colleagues love to say, Mardi Gras is a tradition of times long past, of the ancient rites of spring, when maidens bared their young bottoms and offered their pert breasts to the followers of Pan. Now we will wear our masks, and some men will dress as clowns and some as women; and some women will dress as men; and Blacks will paint their faces white and clip clothespins to their nostrils. We will all ride from house to house to steal chickens. And we will carry our whips of sexual innuendo or intimidation, and we will conduct faux flagellations and mock abductions of womenfolk. We will chase fowl around the yard until we catch them and wring their necks and put them in our soup. Our festivities we will enjoy until the pre-Lent of Ash Wednesday, when we must fast and show our piety.

You know that the Mardi Gras "course" means "race" in French? It is useful to be bilingual in this region, as I am. Do you like my horse? His name is "Fliculate"—FLICK-U-LUT. You may pet his mane or his rump. Do not pet under his tail, because that's where he has the froth of anticipation. He is a fine steed—not a gelding. That's why he is trying to snort up that mare in front of us.

On our horses, with the thunder of ten thousand goats, we ride from house to house, until the capitaine raises his flag. But this is a secret symbol, for in actuality a home-owner requests the Mardi Gras riders, our wondrous gang, to enter his property, to raze the dwelling, to steal his wife and whip his young—*et bien sûr, de chasser les poulets,* to hunt the chickens and wrap thick fingers around their feathery necks and destine plucked white meat for our steaming gumbo supreme. Look! The stout capitaine has lowered the flag. We are welcome in this home. Spur your mount! Gather your flange! Our time is here.

"*Chiquez la paille! Chiquez la paille!*" Chew the straw!

This is what we say when we chase and pretend to pillage. It is an ancient cry from medieval times, a treasured folkloric relic, which we do not fully understand, yet we utter it with gusto and elan, as is our nature. Did you see Monsieur Blanchôt dancing on his horse? He stands in the saddle and waves his arms and stomps his feet. He pretends to unbutton his fly and remove "*son fusil de l'amour*," his love pistol . . . But he does not actually take it out. See! Monsieur Richard (Ree-Shard) has released two chickens from the bathroom door. They cluck and flap their wings. On reddish clawed feet, they wobble and run as they are chased by fat Monsieur Bourgeois, who is very agile, despite his girth. He grabs a Langshan fowl, clamps it between his plump thighs, and twists its tapered neck without allowing its beak near his palms. Let me tell you something—listen to me: a chicken beak is a vicious thing. It can rip into a man's flesh and pierce his genitals. Why do you think the hoodoo *traiteurs* love to put so many beaks in their *conjos*?

Oh yes! The corpulent Bourgeois holds the poultry above his head. He shakes its limp form in victory and waddles with it toward the wagon, the repository of our meat. What is that stream of warm water on my arm? That squirting? Oh, it's nine-year-old Scotty Richard, with his water gun. He wants to get whipped by a clown in a mask, or perhaps by a man in a brassiere. I have my thick whip right here, an oiled black snake. See Scotty's expression of terror and delight as he is walloped? Hear his squeals? His father has locked him out of the house, and now the boy is surrounded, writhing on the grass while the men flagellate him softly. Scotty knows the tradition. He will not be harmed. There will be only mild red marks on his young body, but no bloody gashes, rope burns, or deep bruising; and no blows to the face. Of course, the whipping will stop if the boy grows a boner. Scotty loves this game. It's a wonderful folkloric tradition, better than *Rambo: First Blood Part II*. Mardi Gras will make Scotty a man, and one day he will lock his own son out of the house, to shriek with postured terror, to be mock-whipped by merry marauders in proboscis masks.

Now the neighbors, in front and in back, to the left and the right, have all come to watch Mrs. Richard be abducted. She folds her arms to cover her large breasts, then she releases them. Mrs. Richard is not really shy. She has a lovely figure, and she knows it. She always wears a sleeveless blouse, cut narrow at the waist and wide in the chest. She is being led off by two men in women's dresses, curlers, and wrinkled tights. Their cheeks are colored cherry red with rouge, like silhouette moons of Venus. They wear false eyelashes and black beauty marks the size of dimes—twice as large as deer raisins. Only the most virile men can dress as women. And still, they must make their costumes obvious, with exaggerated busts and makeup, gaudy wigs and fluorescent nails. No man may truly try to appear as a woman—no transsexuals or cross-dressers allowed. They will be beaten. They will not be given any soup.

The men won't harm Mrs. Richard. They really won't even touch her. They won't use their whips on her derrière, or squeeze her privates. They usher her only as far as the driveway, and then release her, with a show of having been tricked into letting her escape. As you see, there are some limits to the Mardi Gras festivity. These parameters are not easily understood by the average citizen. I have studied them for fifteen years, which is why I am such an expert.

Did you notice the women in overalls? The short one with the cigar is Widow Frey. Standing with her are Connie, Sheila St. Jacques, and Fifi LaFleur—all wearing cowboy boots. Fifi is over six feet. She was an all-state volleyball and field hockey champ. Stand aside! The women are coming over. They love to talk to me on these occasions. We speak of many things. I notice they tend to stare at my pants, but I make no remark of this. I am a very reserved person. It comes from my high educational level and academic status. Did you realize that my office is closest to the men's room in the Humanities building? That is because I have seniority.

The Widow Frey is tickling my neck, and suddenly Fifi LaFleur—with her big hands—makes a grab for my crotch (I am not wearing a codpiece). This happened once before. The true significance of this action lies in its folkloric nature. During the reversal allowed in the Mardi Gras festival, the women may become more aggressive than the men. It is permitted. They may enact their autoerotic urges, especially with a subject as knowledgeable as myself—although I must add that women have always found the way I wear my jeans, pulled up high above the navel, quite appealing. "Oh, Doctor Leblanc," says Sheila, "We gonna examine you . . . "

I allow myself to be hoisted up by the four women, each of whom grabs an appendage, a hand or a foot. They carry me around the side of the house, toward the toolshed, to the accompaniment of applause and taunts from the capitaine and his men, plus porcine grunts from Bourgeois, who is pressing up the tip of his nose with his thumb, exposing his nostrils and septum, as if he were actually a hog about to root. (Truthfully, I am at a loss to explain this behavior. It may be concretized ritual embodiment, a remnant of *La Boucherie*, where blood is drained and drunk from larger farm animals.)

The women lug me by all fours, parallel to the ground, sagging at mid-section, and I stare at the yellowing sky. I do not struggle. It is the folklorist's duty not to interfere in the rites of a culture. Thus, I may not alter the course of inversion here, occurring as a function of "festival." I am hauled into the dark toolshed and laid down hard on the concrete floor. My head is underneath a shelf, near a sack of peat moss which I can smell, and which combines in an odd way with the aroma of nutria from the lotion on my thick mustache.

"Doctor, we gotta a sir-prize for you-ou," says Connie Duhon. With my exquisitely developed linguistic sensitivity, I realize that the intonations of Connie's nasal vowels are diphthongic in nature, and thus Connie's "you" rhymes perfectly with "Jew." In fact, at the Tennessee Valley Folklore Conference, I presented a paper, "The Nasal Assonance of Napoleonic Oral Tradition of the Poitou Region," which was extremely well-received.

I am not really surprised when each woman sits on one of my arms or legs and holds me to the floor. Connie and Sheila each sit on one of my calves, and Fifi LaFleur and Widow Frey straddle my arms. Underneath Fifi's overalls, I feel the warmth and dampness of her wide buttocks. I flex my forearm muscle so it bulges beneath her. The women are laughing, cackling really, and Sheila leans over to touch her index finger to my lips. "You just hush now, big Doc. Ain't nobody gonna come get you now . . . "

As a test, to confirm that I could wrench the women off of me and escape if I really wanted to, I try to move my leg, just slide it to the side and simultaneously twist my shoulders, too. I am surprised to find that I am truly pinned in place, held like a cow at the milking machine, with pressure plates against its chest and pelvis and suction cups at its udder. The door to the shed is closed now, and the inner space is lit only by a slice of light from under the roof. The room has a warm, fetid, stagnant odor, like manure in August, and I realize that I am perspiring around my neck and in the clefts beside my groin. The women are oddly quiet, becalmed, as if for the time being they are content merely to sit and gloat about their captive, a practice documented by the explorer Lafcadio Hearn, who was captured by the French and Takapah Indians and then quietly observed. He reported that for several hours, at the beginning of his incarceration, only the words "umbata krendak lahma" ("toad in the hand") were spoken. Later linguistic researchers theorized that the colloquial usage of "umbata . . . lahma," as opposed to the verbial "umbatar," actually connoted the fact that a palm-imprisoned toad will often urinate. This theory has not been fully proven.

Although I am not really frightened, I do decide to use my expertise in oral narratives of escape and take decidedly affirmative action. To distract the women, I drum the fingers of my left hand on an empty tin of paint thinner—I drum pinky, ring finger, middle finger, in that order, as if I am playing the introduction to the bridge of the popular Zydeco folk song, "Toss the Turnips, We Are Late for Church." Yet, covertly, I slide my right arm down toward my waist, near my belt, where hangs the sheath of my Lewis and Clark Signature Replica fish knife, which I mail-ordered from Craftway, Inc. But Sheila St. Jacques has quick reflexes. Her supple arms swing down and her smooth hands grab my own, until Connie extracts the knife from its sheath, and with thumb and forefinger dangles it above my stomach, swinging it to and fro. "Don't you worry 'bout this knife, chère," she says. "We gonna keep it fo' you, nice and safe."

And with that, all the women are laughing again, giggling, until the Widow Frey begins to talk, staring down into my face like a third-grade teacher addressing a disobedient student before administering corporal punishment, raps with a ruler or pantless strokes of a willow switch (both documented in Feodor's classic study, "The Corporeality of the Nascent Urge; Images of Schoolhouse Tradition," for which I was an advisory editor).

"Now Doctor," says the Widow Frey, and as she looks down the length of my reclined body, her three chins contract. "Doc, y'all remember at the Crawfish Festival in Breaux Bridge, when we was tryin' to eat, and you kept lecturin' us on the proper way? You said we had to suck the crawdads' heads, and the thor-axe, 'cause that's what the Indians did. And also chew the feet . . . And then in yer speech, you let on that we were makin' a mistake with the crawfish bisque, because, historically speakin', crawfish were boiled or steamed? Do you remember that, chère?"

I nod my head slowly, but then the widow has grabbed my chin, squeezes my jaw with her fingers, and the sharp curved tips of her artificial nails dig into the skin of my cheeks, making indentations, I'm sure. I have very soft skin.

"You think yer so smart, don'tchee? Don'tchee?" asks Widow Frey, squinting and curling back her lip.

Just then, I feel a hand on my stomach, a steady pressure. With the widow's clasp on my jaw, I can only just barely see Fifi unbuckling my horseshoe belt buckle and unsnapping my pants. I flinch, shiver, but realize that the aggressiveness of these women typifies the inversion of the Mardi Gras rites, and as witness/participant, I must maintain my multi-track aloofness.

Sheila unzips my pants and three women work at once to tug down my jeans and undies. Soon I feel the coldness of the concrete floor on the naked flesh of my hips. Yet I succeed in remaining detached, the mark of a true social scientist. I gaze only at the roof, where the corrugated tin has rusted in a curious half image of the traditional double-swooped butcher's knife, the "grue-grue blade," which was the subject of my doctoral dissertation.

Widow Frey unbuttons my rancho shirt, and now my entire mid-section is exposed, from knees to chest. My genitals are especially prone, yet I make no cry or show alarm. After all, a true festival may not be interrupted, as one of the threads, one of the many fibers which compose the beauty of the rope of folkloric form, will be broken.

From somewhere hidden in the shelving, Connie has procured a tin of Steen's Sugar Cane Syrup, extra-thick, from boiled resin. I blink and feel my forehead wrinkle, always a sign that I am in deep thought. I blink because of the incongruity of this syrup in the shed. While certainly an authentic item of Cajun food ways, its presence clashes with the agricultural folkways of the farm implements, pitchforks and spades, hanging from the walls. This mélange actually reminds me of the syncretism of cultural attributes common in the West African obeahistic spiritualism of this region.

Now Connie is pouring the syrup into her cupped palm. She passes the jar to Sheila, who does similarly. The syrup pours slowly, and finally Sheila hands the jar to Fifi. Then, in ensemble, the three women rub their hands together. The liquid is thick and makes a slapping, almost grating noise with friction. It is applied first to my abdomen, then to my thighs, rubbed in a slow zigzag motion. Six female palms knead my body. I notice that initially the women's efforts seem concentrated on the outer surfaces, the exteriors of my thighs and hips. In fact, this is consistent with the traditional icing of a Creole funnel cake, where molasses is applied to the circumference, before the top—and certainly before the candle is set in place.

At first the women do not touch my male organs. Their hands slide between my thighs and over my umbilicus. The syrup does not harden, yet it doesn't drip, and I feel its continuous presence, its minute tug and suction on my skin. Then Fifi begins to apply the syrup to my testicles. I am able to glance low enough to catch her expression, which is curiously stern and intent, not at all amused or prurient, as she works the length of my male element with two hands. I realize that I am growing erect, a fact which does not slow the smooth circular motions of Fifi's palms; and a fact of which I am not ashamed, as historic folklore often involves bawdy behavior. Yet, truthfully, I would have preferred to leave the stiffness of my sex as an object of idle observation, not the center of attention. But then the Widow Frey leans across me and says, "Old Doc's wood is purty small. Won't make much of a meal . . . "

This remark makes even Fifi grin. I don't have much time to ponder the significance of the word "meal," because just then, the widow has reached into what I now see is an old cloudy-glassed, mold-stained aquarium. There is a flipping smacking noise like fins in water, and suddenly the widow withdraws her arms quickly, holding two animals in her hands. I blink at the writhing multi-legged creatures dangling above my head, and it is with an uncommon hesitation that I realize their species: the Widow Frey is holding two live jumbo spiny crawfish. They are greenish-red, eight inches from head to tail, mandibles and claws intact, antennae wiggling. They make sounds, snapping and clicking noises, tails curling and spreading, fanning the air. I can hear their crustacean hiss, and a few drops of water fall from their bodies onto my neck.

"Now listen ep," says the Widow Frey, staring past the animals into my face. "You think you kin tell us 'bout how to gwon and eat a crawfish? Hell, we been eatin' these damn mudbugs fer a hunnerd years—any way we like 'em! You think you know all 'bout this crawfish? Less see if you know how these *crawfish* eat. We gonna find out, right now . . . "

She sets both animals on my ribcage, where their feet—their eight swimming legs—sink into the coating of syrup which seems to excite them. Their legs scramble in a flurry of motion. Their stalk eyes tremble. One stops for a moment and lowers its head, perhaps to taste the Steen's Syrup, I am not certain. Then it uses its wide fan tail to propel itself forward through the ooze around my navel, toward my groin.

I feel the many sharp feet upon me like light pinpricks, somehow intensified by the gelatinous layer of Steen's; and I observe the asymmetric pincers of the creatures, the larger claw for crushing, the smaller one for cutting and tearing. Crawfish are not unique to Louisiana, yet they have been traditionally prized, even worshipped, especially by the Houma Indians who held them in great esteem as totem animals. The chitinous bodies and calcareous shells feel heavy on my abdomen. The creatures' muscular tails drag and make trails in the ooze. But what I am fascinated by is the index of acculturation in these women's behavior. They have obviously combined the historic laudation of crawfish and Native American vernal crustacean festivities with their own material culture and foodways to create a new tradition, a new ritual to which I, Dr. Hoyt Leblanc, am privy. I must remain alert to all aspects of this ritual, this *fête extraordinaire*, so that I can submit a paper on this topic to the *Southern Folklore Quarterly*, which even in abstract form will no doubt enhance my career.

For some reason, the crawfish have stopped moving. They seem content to rest on my abdomen, claws lowered. Perhaps they are enmired in the syrup—has it interfered with the tendons of the creatures? Or blocked their already minimal neural functions? Perhaps the animals are merely taking a repose, or pausing to communicate. Even the top scientists do not fully understand the language of the animals, you know.

"Git on there!" says Widow Frey. She snaps both crawfish on their tails with her long press-on fingernails, and they jolt forward as if prodded electronically. I realize now that the crustaceans are dangerously close to my penis, which unfortunately is still erect and will provide a greater surface area for the animals to attack, should they misinterpret my phallus as a bloated water worm, or possibly a banana slug. I glance and see that all the women's eyes are focused on the progression of the creatures, as intently as men watching two spurred roosters in a cockfight. Now, it is time for action.

Fortunately, my abdominal muscles are quite developed, as I do sixteen sit-ups per day. Thus I am able to contract my lower stomach rhythmically, creating an undulation of flesh, a ripple of skin, which causes the larger crawfish to lose its balance. It topples off the side of my pelvis where it lies writhing on its back, gooed feet scratching at the air. None of the women touch the spilled crawfish. Silently, they watch its gyrations, and I can hear the rhythmic sound of its shell scraping the concrete. Ksnk, ksnk, ksnk . . .

Aha! So this is the game—a primitive folk test of stamina and inventiveness. I am to find a way to rid myself of these creatures through physical contortion, or perhaps telepathically. Thus, at that moment I close my eyes and concentrate on the mythic forces of nature, the spirits of dead Indians and drowned bayou fisherman to assist me in escaping from the claws of fate of the last crawfish.

But soon Fifi breaks my concentration. "Put 'im back on," she orders. And without flinching, Sheila rights the creature by holding its tail, flipping him, and—pinkie extended as if she were holding an expensive cup of tea—she places the animal upon my thigh. Now I can only see its profile, crenulated and insectoid, and I realize why the early emigrants were at first wary of eating this fierce, spiny animal of the mud.

Both creatures have paused again, hesitating as if uncertain, a few inches from my manhood. Erect, I am seven and seven-sixteenth inches long (18.9 cm), which must pose a curious obstacle to the crawfish. They are completely still, except for twitching antennae. Again, I have an inspiration. I squeeze my sphincter muscle the way I used to practice to prevent premature ejaculation, tightening the muscles of my groin, which has the effect of bobbing the penis slowly up and down, a motion which I hope will frighten the creatures. Unfortunately, it has the opposite effect, and both crawfish move forward simultaneously, their small pincers (for cutting and tearing) snapping and clicking like surreal castanets.

Both crustaceans are now at the base of my stump. And despite my pure objectivity, my scientific detachment and highly developed skills of observation, I find myself clamping shut my eyes and gritting my teeth, awaiting the first piercing grips, the deep incisions. It is my folkloric destiny.

But after a few seconds, dark tense moments in which I feel my entire frame grow rigid and I hold my breath, the crawfish have not begun their attack. They have not drawn blood. Then I feel them move, the larger one first, which grapples through my pubic hair with its swimming feet. Yet it does not begin to eat. I feel its pointed feet, one by one, in a tenuous grip on the vertical surface of my cod. And I soon realize that the animal's objective is motion, not destruction. Step by step, it climbs my stalk, soon followed by the other animal (perhaps its mate), up the other side. They cling to my surface like lizards on a "pieux" fence post, one of the famous holed posts of the Acadian region.

Perhaps I am fortunate that the animals are not hungry. Or have they only mistaken my gender for a birch root bobbing in the swamp; and genetically encoded to do so, they mount the root in search of crickets. Of course, the bark of the birch root has its own traditional significance. Historically used by early settlers as a form of chew, it actually contains a mild stimulant, *stryptocaine*. In the wild, the concentrated exodus of this substance might drift into the water and inspire the animals to mount and climb, to crawl upwards toward the stars, which if observed by Native Americans would provide much needed documentation for the early "Creeper Legends," whose heroes are lowly arthropods which, step by step, grapple for the stars.

Unfortunately, I do not have my tape recorder with me now, so I must suffice with a mental note to research the history of birchwood in folkloric material culture and to trace the evidentiary steps of crawfish lore in palmetto illustrations. Armand Alikkum's desk reference to *fabliaux* of bestiality should provide an adequate cross-index to crustacean practices in pre-Civil War sexual foreplay of the settlers of the waterways of Louisiana. I must not forget these things, I pray to God.

Oh, but the life of a folklore doctor is a difficult, yet wondrous thing . . .

NEANDO

"Have you seen Kimo's drums yet?" asks Tasha. "I'll show you."

I follow her through the garden, past a row of ferns and flowers, and try not to stare at the seat of her jeans. They are ripped at the bottom of one pocket, exposing her naked behind.

A handsome man in a silk paisley shirt steps in our path. "Tasha, love, I haven't seen you lately. Still living in Hollywood?"

"No, I had to get out of there for a while. I'm in Santa Monica now. I wanted some fresh beach air." She emphasizes this by taking in a deep breath and spreads her arms wide. "Listen, I just have to show something to Mark. I'll be right back."

I move to stand closer to Tasha. Then we walk through some crushed gravel behind the house. A metal half-barrel is propped, trough-like, over the remains of a large fire. Inside, in brown water, bobs an oblong wooden shape.

"He's just making that one," says Tasha. "You should have seen the flames, ten feet high, over the roof." She gazes up at the stars. "This is where he keeps the finished ones." She opens a tool shed where twenty or thirty drums are stored: tall African war drums, wide shell-shaped drums, and three tiny hand drums.

I pat the top of a huge Congo drum, waiting for the resonant sound of taut fabric over a hollow space, the satisfying vibration in your stomach—there is only a stiff knock. So I try another, an acrid-smelling little tom-tom, which only clacks—ticks, really. "They don't seem to have the right sound. Are they packed for storage?"

"Oh, Kimo's drums aren't for *playing*. They're for looking."

"They're just for show? They don't make music?"

"Not for 'show.' For *admiration* . . . " She caresses the side of a drum, rubbing two fingers down its shiny joint.

"Cool," I say. What else could you say?

"Very cool . . . " says Tasha, with a serious look.

Seth had invited me to the party, which was supposed to be just for the cast and film crew. I told him I didn't really like that scene, but with one hand on my shoulder, he had assured me that I should go since I was a "hip" writer. Now Seth is inside the house, presiding over the sound system. I watch through the window as he slides in a CD. Watered-down jazz wafts over the speakers. In an instant, the gentle tones of the music, the gray and pink sky of the Venice sunset, and the trendy guests all fuse to form a perfect scene.

I shut my left eye, imagining I am the film camera. I walk from one end of the garden to the other, panning my open eye across the crowd, over the long buffet table, hesitating over a half-full bottle of wine beside a wedge of brie, lingering on Tasha. She stands with two other girls, so similar they may be sisters, paging through an oversized glossy book.

"Oh, Mark, I've been searching all over for you, darling. We were just looking at . . . the book," says Tasha.

"The book?" I glance down at the page—a picture of a pale-skinned woman with puffy lips, perhaps collagen-injected, wearing a short purple hat. "Who's that?"

Tasha twitches, just faintly, and one of the other girls, the tall one, answers in a British accent, "You really don't know who that is?" She turns to her friend and elaborates. "He doesn't know who that is . . . " She pauses for a moment, as if to underscore such terrible lack of knowledge. Finally she speaks. "That's Maude McGraw, of course."

"Mmm, of course," says Tasha. "He knows. He's only teasing."

"Ohh, Tasha," laughs the tall girl, "Do you have the Peter Omert books?"

"Yes, but I lent them to April."

I walk back to the house and bump into Seth—who

almost spills his martini. Expertly, he draws his arm out of the way, switches the drink to his other hand. "How's the party?" he asks, with a quick raise of the eyebrow, the breezy concern of a professional host.

"Excellent. Excellent . . . Listen Seth, actually I have to go soon. I promised my professor I'd have chapter sixteen done by tomorrow," I lie.

Seth shakes his head. "No, Tasha and I are going to take off for a while. Why don't you come along?"

"You're going to leave your own party?"

"A good party is like a Hibachi. You get the charcoal embers going, then you split. It's very hip."

I nod.

"Can we take your car, Mark?" he asks.

I'm proud of my car. A 1965 Dodge Coronet 440 convertible, baby blue with a white leather interior. It has its own class—not the nouveau riche of a Porsche, or the silent pretentiousness of a BMW. The old Dodge has an easy grace.

"This is a great car!" says Tasha. She runs her palm along the chrome fender trim and halfway up the antenna, which she holds between thumb and index finger like a feather.

"Gets me to and from," I answer with the intonation of Black English, the answer I have decided is perfect for car compliments, neither egotistical nor falsely modest.

"Girls in the back," says Seth. He opens the passenger

door, flips forward the bench seat, and Tasha hops in obediently, followed by one of the English girls. "Oh, by the way, I brought our mobile music choice," says Seth. He slips a CD out of his pocket. "If you don't mind." I put in the CD and soon the reverbed, remixed Motown plays on the car stereo. "Now, we're ready," Seth announces.

"We have to go to *Neando*," says Tasha.

"What's Neando?" I ask.

"Oh, it's the only place to go."

"Where is it?"

"West Hollywood, of course. My friend's the bouncer. He always lets me and my other friends in free."

"Groovy."

At Sunset Boulevard, the traffic snags. Seth's quasi-Motown is getting monotonous, as tedious as Muzak—is it Muzak? I keep my eyes on the misty road ahead, and on the dash—the battery gauge shows a discharge. Dammit, another electrical short.

"Everything okay?" asks Seth. He is smiling, beating out the insipid rhythm of the music on his knees.

"Yeah, fine. As soon as we get out of traffic. How far is Neando?"

"Oh, you'll know it when you see it," says Tasha. She gives me a solemn nod.

"Great," I say.

After twenty-five minutes, and no more than three miles, a light rain starts. There is a thin film on the windshield and dampness on the scalp like hair spray. "Is it raining?" asks the British girl.

"No," says Seth. "It doesn't rain in L.A."

Tasha wipes the moisture from her brow.

"We better put up the top, so the leather will be all right." I turn into a liquor store parking lot. I get out and lean over to lift up the convertible top. Then I feel a smooth hand on my abdomen, fingers rubbing in little circles.

"Mark, will you buy me some tequila?" asks Tasha. "I always drink before Neando. They always let me bring the bottle inside." She gazes up at me with bottomless violet eyes.

"Let's keep moving," says Seth. He reaches into his blazer pocket, pulls out two small airline bottles of Johnny Walker Red, and hands them to Tasha.

The rain grows heavy, falls in sheets—a fusillade of drops. I put the wipers on full speed. They don't swing parallel like modern wipers. The motion of each blade is a mirror image of the other. In noisy arcs, their tips meet at the center of the windshield.

The discharge gauge shows more power loss. The dashboard lights are growing dim, so I shut off the headlights at every intersection to save the battery. No one speaks. Seth stops drumming. Everyone is still, motionless as wax figures. Then Tasha screams, "NEANDO! I see it. FUCKING GOD! I see it! There's Neando!"

A line of people, most dressed in black, stretches around the block like a quintessential gangland funeral procession, *à la* Metro Goldwyn Mayer 1949. Above a small door, battered and plastered with torn posters, is the single word *NEANDO* written in a stylized, faux Greek script.

"Let me out! I'll go talk to the bouncer," says Tasha. She rolls down the back window and—wriggling her shoulders, writhing her torso—tries to squirm out.

"Just wait." I pull over and swing open the door. Tasha squeezes out and springs into the rainy street, swinging her hips like Brigitte Bardot, drawing a fluttering hand through her hair. She is oblivious to the passing cars, which somehow avoid hitting her with a drone of horns and screech of brakes.

The car behind us keeps honking, inching closer and closer as if the risk of collision will inspire me to move. So we drive around the block, a giant warehouse district littered with crushed paper cups. Back in front of Neando, Tasha seems to be arguing with the fat bouncer. She leans forward and thrusts out her jaw. Then she whirls around and stomps back to the car. Seth pulls seat forward to let her in.

"Well?" he says.

Tasha doesn't answer. I glance in the rearview mirror.

Those aren't raindrops on her cheeks; they're tears. "Was there a problem?" I ask softly.

"The bastard wouldn't let me in. There's some private party or something."

"We'll find another club."

"There aren't any others," she snorts and glares at me.

"Well, surely in Los Angeles, there might be one or two other night clubs . . . " I say, and glance at Seth, who is expressionless, hands clasped over his lap.

Tasha grabs the seat with two hands and shouts at me, "You don't understand! All my friends are in there. In there!" She starts to cry again—two perfect single streams of tears run down her cheeks. The British girl pets her shoulder.

Seth speaks in a low voice. "Let's just go home."

The traffic eases up, but the rain still falls in heavy leaden layers, resonating off the convertible top like the pounding of the surf. A small hole drips water onto Tasha's back. She doesn't seem to notice. At every traffic signal, I turn off the headlights again and watch the dashboard lights flicker. Then Tasha kicks my seat—"You don't have to keep doing that with the lights!" She shakes her nose.

A flush of anger rises in my neck, and there is a bristling in my forearms. But I answer in a controlled voice, "Frankly, Tasha, I do . . . You see, the headlights consume an enormous amount of electricity, and at a stop, the

RPMs aren't high enough to charge the battery and make up for the drain."

"Jesus! This is the worst night of my life," she groans. Then suddenly, no longer sad, curiously adamant, she slaps my head rest. "Put on the radio!"

I slam on the brakes and twist to face her. The seat back separates us like a pigpen wall. "Listen, Tasha, I'm sorry you didn't get to Neando Mecca. And I'm sorry the electrical system has a problem, but we can't listen to the radio. The car will stall. Sing a song if you want."

Seth smiles a little.

"I'm not going to sing a fucking song."

"All right. I'll sing a song. Shall I sing a song, Tasha?" I clear my throat. "Here . . . " I wait for a moment, a dramatic microsecond, then begin in a deep baritone that got me the lead in the high school musical:

> Oh, say can you see
> By Neando's dim light . . .

"Shut up," says Tasha.

But I continue, drawing out my syllables from the diaphragm, like Pavarotti.

> Where so soundly we failed
> At the bouncer's redeeming . . .

A huge blast of thunder pounds and crashes through the sky.

"God. What was that?" asks the British girl.

"The great spirit of Kimo's drums," I answer. "Come to haunt us."

The rain beats down on the vinyl roof. Hard pellets of rain. But now the battery is charging again; there is a quiver of the white indicator needle, and the dash lights have brightened in a pulse of energy. Somehow, the car has found a way to recharge itself.

I take a chance and turn on the radio, preset to a classical station. Soon the delicate piano notes of Bach's *Goldberg Variations*, complete with Glenn Gould's moans, spread through the car in a comforting but surreal manner. The music seems just the right frequency to drown out the sound of the rain.

Tasha exhales through her teeth, a thin bitter noise. "Let me out."

Seth is silent.

The British girl gasps.

I pull over again, open the door, and Tasha exits the car. For a moment she is alone on the corner, the rain beating down on her T-shirt so it clings to her chest, water streaming through her hair so it glistens. She stands there, akimbo, a perfect wet maiden.

But she isn't there long. In the rearview mirror, I watch her flag down a Mercedes. Its driver, with muscular arms and a surgeon's collarless green shirt, leans over to unlock the door. Then Tasha is kissing his cheek. Glowing.

I wheel the big Dodge down a side street, a spray of road wash in our wake. But to the South, the skies are clearing. Serene blue light shows through. I turn up the radio volume all the way.

Bach's *Goldberg Variations* resound inside the car—trinkling, technical, triumphant . . .

A TASTE OF HEAVEN

There were rumors going around about applesauce.

In Trailer 6 at Oasis Mobile Estates, Dorothy Johnson ran hot water on the rim of a big economy jar of Seneca unsweetened applesauce. Today she was wearing her new *Easy Care Maiden Stretch-O-Matic* sky-blue slacks and matching blue-striped peach melba blouse. From the unused back bedroom with plastic rosewood paneling, behind the shoe boxes filled with Campbell's Soup wrappers and wine bottle corks (mostly from André Cold Duck, her favorite, which she mixed with grape Tang), in front of the towering twin stacks of *Reader's Digest* magazines—all missing the "Word Power" page, which she always snipped out and kept in a drawer in the kitchen next to a Quaker Oatmeal canister that actually contained hundreds of plastic kiddie toys taken from cereal boxes, still in their cellophane envelopes. In the midst of all this, Dorothy found her collection of Gerber Baby Food jars (five hundred and eleven), individually wrapped in newspaper like Christmas tree ornaments. She carried the jars into the kitchen and set them on the counter until she had seventeen jars, all with the labels carefully soaked off years ago.

Dorothy filled each jar with a big serving of glistening pulpy yellow applesauce and stuck in a plastic spoon. The Johnson Club was meeting at 2:30 pm. Dorothy was president. She had decided that would be their secret communal food, their Eucharist. Four months ago, the *National Enquirer* had run a story about how Elvis learned from aliens that applesauce was the purest form of nourishment available on earth, not potatoes as commonly believed. Potatoes had too much sodium. Applesauce was Elvis' dream food, his rejuvenation potion. He was eating only applesauce every day and living in India until his miraculous second coming in the year 2019, when he would look exactly like he did in that Hawaiian movie. Dorothy had a glossy lavender velvet painting of Elvis—head, open shirt, smooth chest, guitar—hanging in her living room. She used to have a picture of Jesus on the cross, too, but she took it down the year Barack Obama got elected. Now there was only Elvis.

The Johnson Club would eat their applesauce, their healthful "eudaemonic" (a word which came directly from "Word Power," and Dorothy was happy to master it). The club deserved only the best. It had rigorous membership qualifications and formed an elite group. To be a member, your last name had to be "Johnson." Dorothy had advertised the club in the *Oasis Gazette* and put up a sign at the Dairy Mart, on the bulletin board near the eggs. She had seventeen official fully registered Johnsons. Of course, they had already paid their fifty-dollar annual fee which covered, among other things, weekly applesauce nutriment and the cost of an orange club beret (Dacron and Rayon—wool was too hot) with a black "J" sewn on the top.

Suddenly Dorothy was hungry. Ravenous. With a quick prefatory check to make sure no one was peeking in her trailer windows, she stuck two curved fingers into the neck of the applesauce jar, scooped out a big mound of the "extra pulpy" sauce, and put it in her mouth.

Trailer 37 was a 1959 Camperlux Twin with fins, round "space age" porthole windows, and a curved aerodynamic roof. But over the years, the metal window frames had rusted and the bulbous roof had become caked with sticky brown resin from the tire retread plant two blocks away. Strands of adhesive gum wafted through the air in pollen-sized particles which descended and set in a layer on top of the trailer like tar, unless scrubbed off immediately. Hundreds of fallen oak leaves also stuck to the roof and sides of Trailer 37, so now it looked more like an abandoned barnacled submarine than any surface dwelling.

Frank Deal, a.k.a. Frank Deloatch, a.k.a. "Spackle," didn't care about his rusty window frames. In fact, as he tottered around in a pair of dungarees that he washed once a month, and a flannel shirt that he washed once a week, Frank didn't think much about the age or the odor of his trailer at all. In 1975, he had burned the registration papers—soaked them in kerosene and ignited them in the oven—so no one could prove that the coach was older than 1963, the park limit. Frank had a lot on his mind. He had just discovered the second secret ingredient for his wonder product, "Nu-Crete." It would make him the richest man in the world.

On Tuesday night, Herb Johnson, a.k.a. "Herd," had come over with two bottles of Wild Turkey that he won at the raffle, one tucked under each of his arms. Given the proximity to Herd's underarms, at first Frank wasn't sure that he wanted to drink the whiskey. Herd's nickname was based on the smell of the pungent "Vinaigrette Cooler" combination aftershave / antiperspirant / cologne that he bought ten cases of in 1983, part of a special deal when the company was going out of business. Herd had determined to wear the cologne until he ran out to get all his money's worth, despite that fact that people thought the cologne smelled of wet dog. But in the end, since the bottles were sealed, Frank had decided the whisky might still be okay to drink.

They sat at Frank's kitchen table. Frank started talking about "Nu-Crete"—or saying as much as was safe to tell. "You know, Nu-Crete's a hunnerd times stronger than ordinary cee-ment," said Frank. "That's cause of the secret 'gredient I went and added to the mix. It bonds them molleecules all tight. Snug as a bug." He chuckled and poured a big splash more Wild Turkey into a chipped coffee cup. "I went and got what they call a poor man's patent on my formula. Now a' course, Herd, I can't go and tell you about the secret 'gredient and all, but I supppose it's safe to let on that I rented a safety box dee-posit at the bank in Barstow. Every sixth Friday, I take a bus on up there to check the envelope. To make sure it's all right. No mites or nothin' . . . And no spy eyes itchin' to learn the mystery and take all my money!" Frank pounded his fist on the table. And burped.

Herd turned away, switched on the television to re-runs of *Wheel of Fortune*, and tried to guess the "Famous Phrase":

__U C K__ __EVEN

"Vanna never even washes her face," said Frank. "That's cause, see, she's got a special bionic organic layer." He leaned forward, pressed four fingers against the side of his mouth as if to prevent eavesdropping, and whispered, "A *Nu-Face* . . . "

Herd snorted. He sat way back in his chair, lifting it on two legs, almost tipping it over. "Down at the Johnson Club, we got a secret potion, too. A 'juvenation formula. For bowels and kidneys and all." He gave a sly nod and couldn't resist a wink, too. "It's a health food, a miracle curer—only I can't tell you what it is, Frank. It's a club secret. Members only," Herd laughed, and measured out three fingers more Wild Turkey. "I can tell you this, though. Totie Johnson already proved it works. Clinched it. She told us at the meeting. Her son, Lathe—you know the one with the Mohawk hair-do? Well, he had a bashful bladder. See, Lathe couldn't ernate—"

"What?" asked Frank.

"Ernate—piss . . . Lathe couldn't piss in front of his mother for his drug tests. So Totie gave him some of the secret health potion and it smoothed him out. It's the same stuff we all take at the Johnson Club. So Totie told President Johnson just how good it worked. And President Johnson—Dorothy—made us all say, 'One, two, three, smooth' before we ate the first spoonfuls. And we had to swallow together, too."

Of course Herd could see that Frank was getting pretty curious now. His eyes had narrowed and were starting to gleam. Then Frank scoffed, rubbed his neck, and wouldn't look at Herd. Frank turned to watch Vanna on TV. He watched her clap every time the giant wheel of fortune spun; he saw her wiggle like a mermaid in a long green sequined dress, cut low at the bust line. He imagined Vanna was clapping just for him—the way she would when he had a Nu-Crete empire . . . Frank licked his bottom lip. "Well, what kind a Johnson potion y'all got over there anyway?" he asked, making sure he sounded casual, as if he only wondered what septic tank chemical they used.

"I can't tell you. Members' honor."

Frank grunted. Then he clucked his tongue against his teeth. Finally he stood up and, as if he were opening a jewelry box, slid out the bottom kitchen drawer and pulled forth a paper which he pressed close against his chest.

"What's that?" Herd felt the heat in his face, flushed with Wild Turkey.

"Here . . . " Frank handed out the paper, held it fluttering in the air. "It's the Nu-Crete motto. I decided I can trust you on that."

Herd glanced down. The hen-scratched letters were mostly capitals with lower-case "t's":

IF YOUR DRIVEWAY AIN't NU-CREtE, It's SHIt.

Herd flipped the paper over. Maybe Frank had forgotten, and written the secret Nu-Crete ingredient on the back . . . No such luck.

Frank guzzled the last of the liquor right out of the bottle. "All rightee. I decided I'll let on about my Nu-Crete 'gredient, if you tell about the Johnson juice, or whatever."

Herd wasn't anybody's patsy. He knew how these things worked, how intricate these negotiations could be. "You tell first," he said.

Frank leaned forward and put a hand on the edge of a

chair to steady himself. "Elmer's Glue All!" he hissed. Then he snapped his bumpy wiry frame upright. His eyes were wide, bulging as if he had just seen a scorpion on the shelf. "Now you tell!" he almost shouted. "Come on there!" His voice cracked.

Herd hesitated for a moment, just long enough to make Frank stomp his foot and squirm. Then Herd spoke slowly, over-enunciating each syllable. "Applesauce." Herd's stomach twisted, he felt a dagger in his gut—he had just violated the sacred covenant of the Johnson Club. He had just lost the right to wear his beret proudly. Then he shivered when Frank wrote out the word "applesauce" on his own sweaty palm with a red permanent marker.

"Now I got 'gredient number two!" Frank glowed. He smiled and showed a row of nicotine-stained teeth. "Hah!" His chin trembled.

In Trailer 52 in the back of the park, Skat Turner sat outside with Les Thoms and Pete Tarpus. All three of them held well-oiled CO2 BB guns across their knees. The rifles glistened in the afternoon sun. Skat was president of the "T" club, which had only been in existence three weeks. Originally, Skat had wanted to join the Johnson Club after his neighbors, Floyd and Totie Johnson, had joined, and kept talking about how much fun it was. "Slicker than a night crawler in manure," is what Floyd had said. So Skat asked Floyd to ask President Johnson if he could join as a special category member. But she said "No"—only *Johnsons* were allowed. Then Skat offered to change his last name to "Johnson," officially, at the courthouse and all. But President Johnson still said "No"—only "authentic Johnsons" would be accepted.

So Skat made a plan.

He put up signs at the True-Value Hardware, the 7-11, and at the Rexall Drugstore. These were cardboard posters advertising for members to join the new "Turner" Club.

But no one applied for membership.

So Skat changed the name to the "T" club. Anyone with a last name beginning with "T" could join. But he got only two responses—from Les and Pete, so there didn't seem to be much point in having any formal club meetings. Now when Les and Pete came over, the three T-club members just sat around and shot bottles and jars with BB guns. And they drank root beer.

Les raised his rifle, fit the butt against his shoulder, sighted down the long steel-blue barrel, pulled the trigger softly, and let whiz a streaking humming BB that shattered a small glass jar over by the fence.

"Nice one," said Pete. He took a final gulp of root beer, rubbed the sweat from his forehead, and aimed at a Pepsi can near the bushes. But just then, a big monarch butterfly with gold and black wings etched like lace floated down gently and fluttered to the grass at the edge of the fence.

Pete swung his rifle barrel toward it . . .

Skat kicked Pete with a pointy-toe-cowboy-boot kick that caught Pete in his flabby rear end, which extended in a roll over the side of his folding chair. "No shootin' wildlife, Pete. Otherwise you'll be outta the club," said Skat.

"Ah wasn't gonna shoot. I was jus' checkin' the . . . "

Tires scraped across the driveway and Kathleen Turner, Skat's wife, pulled up in her 1989 Buick Estate Wagon. She banged open the door and set one of her Hush-Puppied feet out, then the other. She grabbed a plastic shopping bag, jolted out of her seat, and slammed the car door shut. She tossed back her hair with the quick swivel of the neck that she always fashioned when she was angry. Skat knew the swivel well. After a few moments, Skat's twelve-year-old son, Skeeter, opened the rear door of the Wagon and scampered around his mother into the trailer, where he turned on the TV. Soon the quacking, bleating "Beep Beep" of a *Road Runner* cartoon was almost louder than Kathleen's demand: "Gimme the rifle, Skat. I'm mad." She kicked at an innocuous clod of dirt.

Skat spoke in a soft voice. "What's wrong, honey? How was the—"

"Just gimme the rifle quick. I'm in a shootin' mood!" she snapped, and took a single calculated step forward like advancing infantry. Slowly Skat stood up, dragged his tall six-foot-three-inch frame off of a stack of tires and, barrel to the ground, handed his wife the BB gun. Les and Paul stood up too. They stepped back off the grass, almost out into the driveway, just as Kathleen let fly with a blazing round of BB fire that pinged and ricocheted and sent the lid of the broken glass jar skipping toward the fence; sprang the Pepsi can a full two feet in the air; thrust little mounds of earth and grass up like miniature land mines; and left the butterfly perfectly safe, if not oblivious, a few yards away.

"Good shootin," said Les. He let out a low whistle.

But Kathleen wasn't listening. She dropped the rifle in the grass, let it slip from her hands to the ground. "You know who I saw today?" she asked, her brow wrinkling, head quivering, jaw clenched like a C-clamp. She stalked over to Skat. "You know who was at the market today? Totie Johnson—that's who . . . And when I went over to say hello, Totie just pushed her cart away real fast. And she yelled at me not to look in her cart because she was buying secret stuff for the Johnson Club." Kathleen hung her head. "And she wouldn't even talk to me."

Skat hesitated before answering, stood up straighter, then spoke carefully, swallowing the ends off his words, keeping his emotion at bay. "What was in the basket?"

Kathleen just shook her head, shrugged, closed her eyes and wiggled her chin as if purging the question, the very thought, from her mind. "I have no idea."

"SKEETER!" Skat roared, "Come on out here, son." Skat forced his words over the din of the *Road Runner* theme.

Skeeter opened the screen door and poked his tow-head outside the trailer. His lips were bright red, fluorescent cherry, from the artificial coloring in Hawaiian Punch. In his hand he held a stack of Oreo cookies. Proudly, Skat looked at his son's face—the son who worked a hard day at school and came home for a snack, a good American God-fearing snack of punch and cookies. "Son, do you know what a 'mission' is?" asked Skat in a deep, low voice.

Skeeter nodded. "Sure. That's where the priests go. Where they keep the guns n' stuff to fight Indians."

"Yes. Very good. Do you know what else it is?"

Skeeter shook his head, rubbed his nose and, with a vacant stare, took a whole cookie in his mouth.

"A mission is when a soldier has a duty. When a man has a, a quester."

"*Quest,*" Kathleen whispered, but Skat ignored her. He glanced over at Les and Pete standing somber and pious at the edge of the driveway, hands in their pockets, BB rifles leaning against the car, both taking in Skat's words like a sermon.

"Yes," Skat continued with an even deeper resonance in his voice, allowing it to entrance his audience. "It is a quester, Skeeter." Skat stepped forward. "Now come on over here, son. You, have, a mission." And with that, Skat leaned down to whisper into his boy's ear, a whisper that none of the spectators could hear but surely they surmised—a whisper of potions and meetings, of secrets and spies, of information and intrigue... Neither Pete Tarpus nor Les Thoms heard these words, nor Kathleen herself, but certainly they saw the strong hunched shoulders of Skat Turner, noted the wide and serious eyes of little Skeeter, his periodic nods . . . And they knew the mission must involve—the quest would surely entail—covert operations against the Johnsons!

On Thursday afternoon at three when the Johnsons had their meeting, Skeeter was not at baseball practice. He was not playing pinball at the arcade. He was not at his friend's house sneaking peeks at his friend's dad's *Playboy* magazines from the 1950s, when the girls still wore tights . . . No, Skeeter was high in the oak tree above Trailer 6. Above Dorothy Johnson's trailer.

Skat had told Skeeter exactly what to do. How to spy on the meeting through the air vent on the trailer roof to see just what-in-hell the Johnsons were doing in there. To find out what their secret food was . . . Now Skeeter pulled his skinny body along the crooked sloping bough of the tree that grew over the trailer. The going was tough. Sharp bits of bark dug into Skeeter's thigh—he shouldn't have worn shorts—and a trail of red ants, piss ants, ran along the bough. Piss ant bites stung and burned—Skeeter knew that. And the piss ants smelled like pee if you popped them. Skeeter brushed two red ants from his arm. He didn't pop them.

Inching his way along the branch like a caterpillar, straddling the limb with his weight slightly off-center so the bough didn't press into his groin, Skeeter tugged himself along. When he got halfway out, his body weight made the big branch sag so it was only a five-foot drop, not far, to the top of Dorothy's trailer. Skeeter grasped the bough with two arms—hugged it as hard as he could—and let his legs pivot and unwrap from the bough all the way until his feet kicked in thin air and, finally, one toe touched the roof of the trailer, then the other. Skeeter eased his weight onto the roof—ball of foot, sole, heel—and dropped gently into a crouching position. He was safe.

Dorothy washed her trailer often. She hired a special washing truck and crew with an air compressor pump and a mist gun. They sprayed the sides and roof of her trailer and left their bill hanging from the door handle. Skeeter had watched them many times. But still there was a film of brown gum from the tire plant coating the louvered top of the trailer, and it stuck to Skeeter's knee and to the toes of his sneakers. It clung to his palms like paste as he slithered over the trailer roof. Skeeter had to stay low-profile, stomach down, so no one would see him. But then the tarry resin stained his shirt, too. He couldn't show his mother that. He would have to get his dad to buy him a new shirt. After all, Skeeter was on this mission for his father, right? Skat had told him the mission was for the "better res'dents" of the park.

Skeeter was quiet, yes, very quiet as he inched over to the air vent and peeked down at the Johnson meeting. He blinked a few times. From his vantage point overlooking the living room, he saw a field of orange circles, bright orange. They looked like frog eggs floating in a mass at the edge of a pond. Skeeter leaned closer, pressing his forehead against the cool metal rim of the vent. Then he could see shoulders, people standing side-by-side, elbow to elbow, and the orange circles—these were some kind of funny hats, flat saucer hats . . . There was a letter on the top of each hat—why hadn't he seen that before? A letter stitched right in the middle of each orange saucer: "J." Scores of J's standing together. And then, at the same moment, in a blur of cognition, a coalescence of educational experience and sacred duty, a flash of understanding hit Skeeter that sent a shiver down his spine. He knew what the "J's" stood for . . . He had read about them at Sunday school. These were Judaics!

What were they doing? Skeeter watched, peered, gawked, as Dorothy—he could see her funny horn-rimmed glasses—squeezed between each row of people and gave out little glass jars with plastic utensils sticking out. The jars were passed from hand to hand. They were baby food jars . . . The Johnsons were eating baby food! Skeeter had to tell his father that he had discovered their secret! Solved the mystery! Mission accomplished. But just then, part of the curved metal roof sunk and caved in under Skeeter's knee on which he had been resting all his weight. The roof cracked, depressed like an egg carton when you step on it. Underneath him, Skeeter heard something drop and shatter. Something large and glass. He heard a female's scream—was that Dorothy? Then there was a male voice yelling, "SOMEBODY'S THERE! SOMETHING IS UP THERE!"

Skeeter wasn't thinking now. His chest thudded, jolted, as he crawled—crab-scrambled—for the edge of the roof. He swung his legs over the side of the trailer as fast as he could. He didn't even feel the gash from a sharp screw cutting deep into his shin. As he jerked his legs over the side, the ridged edge of the roof dug hard into his stomach. And it hurt. But holding on with his elbows, kicking his feet, Skeeter wiggled toward the back of the trailer—then his right foot crashed into a glass window. He heard it shatter, heard the sickening tingle of glass shards falling onto the trailer floor.

Inside the trailer, there was another curdling scream, higher-pitched this time, and many stomping feet. The sides of the trailer shook and rocked as Skeeter dropped to the pavement. The impact sent spearing pains through his knees, but he didn't stop. He turned and ran. He didn't look back. He sprinted away in effortless floating steps, faster than a horse, faster than wind. He tore around the back of the cul-de-sac, jumped over a tiny hedge, galloped back beside the big chain-link fence at the perimeter of the park and, finally, he stopped. He was trembling, gasping—which way? He headed straight ahead—no time for lengthy decisions. He wheeled around and darted into the bathroom near the laundry building. The filthy bathroom that no one ever used.

It was dark inside, damp and moldy. It smelled like a thousand-year-old toilet. An inch of water covered the concrete floor. Skeeter could hear it lap at his feet as he walked deeper into the bathroom toward the back wall. Finally, he laid both hands flat on the cracked tile wall and took a deep breath. His throat ached. He closed his eyes and inhaled through his nose in burning streams of air. Now the cut on his shin throbbed and stung. That screw had dug in deep. Skeeter gasped, choked—A sweaty arm wrapped around his throat, and a hand grabbed his hair, jerked back his head. Skeeter froze. He didn't even breathe.

Then the hand slowly released Skeeter's hair and took his shoulder in a taloned clutch which swung Skeeter around. The arm slid from Skeeter's neck. Two hands held him at the collar bone, pressed him against the wall, and he stood there staring up into a mottled leering face with sharp, gray hawk-eyes. It was Spackle-Frank Deal . . .

"What are you doin' in here, boy?" Frank's voice was hoarse, almost a cough. "Why are you runnin' out there? Answer me!"

Skeeter's knees were numb. He couldn't feel his feet. He gazed up into the oily quivering face of Frank Deal, stared at his bony forehead and long greasy hair. Skeeter blinked. He wanted to lie. His mind churned, flashed—he had to think of a story, a reason . . . His mouth had dropped open and he closed it. He didn't know what to say. He couldn't think. So he told the truth, with a quavering voice. His arms shook. "I, I was on the trailer, and I heard—on top, I mean. On the roof. Dorothy's roof." Skeeter swallowed hard. "I was spying on the meeting, to see the secret stuff and—"

"See what?" Frank squeezed Skeeter's shoulder like a vice grip. A dot of spittle stuck to his lower lip. "The secret what?"

Skeeter had stopped trembling. He glanced at the cool blue light filtering in from top of the door, cutting a bright triangle through the darkness. "I was trying to find out the Johnson secret. Their food, you know?"

Now Frank was shaking. His Adam's apple, a bony pointed thing, jerked up and down on his long thin throat. "What was it?" he hissed. His eyes narrowed, but got brighter too somehow. "What were they eatin'?"

"I saw . . . " Skeeter glanced again at the door, which had swung ajar. He could see the rocky asphalt path outside . . . "I saw baby food."

"Unh?" Frank snarled. He leaned back—but then Skeeter charged. He lowered his head and shoulders and rammed past the sweaty Frank, shoulder-shoved under Frank's ropy arms, and dashed outside into the sunlight. He ran down the back path like a wild squirrel. He kept running while his chest burned and swelled until he was all the way out of the trailer park. Until he was down the street, over the fence, through the wild brush, and safe in the drainage ditch under the intersection where he and his friends always hid from police; where they had a good supply of rocks and sharp sticks for protection. Where Skeeter was secure.

Careful not to touch a clump of poison oak, Frank Deal squatted like a defecating camper in the bushes next to Trailer 10. He tried to quiet his wheezing breath, the only sound except for a bird pecking somewhere in the trees above. With a savage tug, Frank broke off a twig that was blocking his view as he gazed into the streaked glass window of the trailer. He spied into the kitchen. Hunched over the sink, a can opener in his hand, stood Herd Johnson—the liar. The bastard. The rat-fink. Herd had conned Frank, tricked him. He told Frank that the secret Johnson food was "applesauce." But it wasn't—it was baby food. The kid saw it . . . Baby food was the special nutriment. And goddammit, Frank had traded away his sacred Nu-Crete formula for a lie!

Frank swiveled his neck and twisted his head to fit it sideways between the branches of a bush. The leaves tickled at his ears like crawling insects, but now he could get a better view of the lumpy paunchy Herd Johnson—what was Herd doing? He was opening a can, a Sheeba Gourmet Cat Food can . . . With a big serving spoon, Herd scooped the meat into a bowl, chopped at it with the side of the spoon, ran the spoon under the faucet for a moment and—what was that big jar? Seneca Applesauce! Herd was mixing applesauce with the cat food! Must be a big joke, huh? Telling him about applesauce-catfood, instead of telling the truth . . .

Frank pressed down his stiff knees and raised himself into a half-crouch. Then he stood upright. His thighs were tight from squatting. The sharp twigs from the brush had poked him, made him itchy, and he rubbed a palm against his leathery neck, using the dirt on his hand as an abrasive. The itch felt hot like a rash. Just then a hairy animal darted past Frank into the bushes! He barely saw it. But it was big, like a fox, or a coyote. Maybe a stray dog. Maybe rabid . . .

Frank patted his pocket for the outline of his knife, a giant thirty-six-blade Swiss Army knife. An authentic one, from Germany. He pulled it out and opened the first tool that his thumb landed on—the scissor blade. Then, with the scissors clutched out in front of him, holding his breath, Frank took a step forward into a crackle of dry leaves, through a swathe of bushes, and there! Next to the rock pile. It wasn't a coyote—it was a cat. An enormous furry cat, at least thirty pounds, brown, with wide eyes. It sat crouching there, relaxed really, blinking up at Frank, watching him with clear glowing topaz cat eyes that didn't waver. Then the cat meowed.

This wasn't a snarling meow. Certainly not a growling meow. It was a throaty whelp of a meow, a low-pitched greeting as only a huge Maine Coon cat can muster. And Frank knew he was out of danger. He clicked the scissors away and slipped the knife back into his pocket. He stared at the plump cat, which wasn't the least bit frightened, and even stretched, pushing forth two round fuzzy padded feet, extending its claws, stretching out its neck, raising its furry bottom, flexing and arching down its legs. Then it meowed again.

Herd's voice came from his trailer. "BUHHH-TERRR . . . Here kitty. Come on, Butter. Time for special secret dinner . . . " Through the brush, Frank saw Herd lean out the window and crane his neck around, twisting his big head back and forth. There he was! Head exposed. The conniving Nu-Crete ingredient-learner! The applesauce liar!

All of a sudden, Frank's jaw tightened, his cheeks tensed. He squinted his eyes half-closed for protection, bent low, ran forward through the bushes, and grabbed Herd's cat. He snatched Butter up in two arms. The heavy thing was almost as big around as a person, and Frank held the cat tight—squeezed hard so it couldn't scratch or bite—lucky he had worn his thick Levi's jacket . . . But the cat didn't try to claw. Butter didn't want to bite. The immensely hairy animal wrapped its two front legs around Frank's neck, laid its head on Frank's shoulders, right under his chin, and began to purr.

This was no ordinary purr. It was a loud outboard motor of a purr, a puffing croaking purr. And as Frank plodded through the brush, sneaking and slinking along by the fence line, he barely heard his own footsteps over the loud purrs of the cat . . . Then Butter began to lick Frank's jaw with a warm, sandpaper-tongued lick. Frank tried to hold the cat out, to thrust it forward out of reach of licks. The fur was so thick that Frank couldn't even see his own hands through the hair. Butter purred even louder. And amidst continuous licking and occasional ecstatic meows, Frank carried Herd's gargantuan cat back to his rusted submarine of a trailer. Then he locked Butter in the bathroom.

OASIS MOBILE ESTATE WEEKLY GAZETTES

"A Taste of Heaven in the West"

* FRANK DELOATCH from Trailer 37 has received a $100 reward for locating Herb Johnson's lost cat, "Butter." Frank said, "Butter is a good cat 'cause he ain't got no hairballs." Frank plans to use his reward money for an

upcoming trip to Las Vegas.

* HERB JOHNSON has announced that "only those persons with clean hands" will be allowed to pet Butter from now on.

* According to DOROTHY JOHNSON, Johnson Club meetings will be suspended indefinitely due to an outbreak of food poisoning which has affected many club members.

* SKAT TURNER, T-Club president, wants everyone to know that he has received thirty-two new applications for membership. 'We're cookin'," says Skat. The T-Club still has room for three more members. Contact Skat at Trailer 52. Bring your own BB gun.

* Congratulations! 12-year-old SKEETER TURNER has won his school's Jungle Survival Training Contest. "All I did was the natural," said Skeeter.

* Trailer 11 is vacant and available now. GOOD SAMARITANS with current resident referral only. Apply at the Park Office.

AND THAT'S ALL THE NEWS THAT COUNTS!

This Week's Phrase:
"To get to heaven, turn *right*, then eat an apple a day . . . "

I BOUGHT A BOOK

I bought a book. Books are good. Amazon sent it to my house. That was nice. I read my book. I liked it. I wanted to tell the world about my reading experience. Amazon let me review my book. That was nice. I typed my review, and Amazon flashed me a message that my review was submitted. That was nice.

I kept checking to see my review online. I waited three days to see my review. It never showed up. I typed the review again and submitted it. Amazon thanked me for submitting. After two days, the new review hadn't appeared. I typed and submitted it again. But that didn't work.

I thought about the possible reason why Amazon did not want my review. Perhaps it might have something to do with the Germanic name that I had used as a pseudonym to submit the review. I use a pseudonym because I don't want a seller to get angry and track me if I write something bad. I use a German pseudonym, "Hartmut."

(I like to pronounce the vowels in Germanic names.)

I suspected that Amazon might not like my Germanic name since it did not match the name on my credit card. So I changed my Amazon name to a closer version of my actual name, even though the syllables are not as fun to pronounce. I submitted the review again. Amazon thanked me. I waited two days. The review did not appear.

I began to research possible reasons why my review was not posted online. I read reports on seller sites and Reddit. Apparently, Amazon is getting very suspicious about whether or not a reviewer is a friend of the author. There is speculation that Amazon is sniffing IP addresses and social media sites to try and determine if a reviewer is a friend of the author, and rejecting reviews on that basis. I am a friend of the author of my book.

My name is Hartmut. I am a friend of the author of my book.

I emailed the author and told him that our friendship might be a reason for why my review was not being posted on Amazon. The author disagreed. The author felt that the reason Amazon did not like my review was that I used a fake German name to post the review, and this concerned Amazon. I explained that I had temporarily tried to switch to a version of my real name to submit the review, but that didn't work either . . . The author suggested that I submit a review about a different product, so that we could diagnose the extent of the review posting problems. I did not want to do that because I had a headache.

I lay down and decided to contact customer service at Amazon about the issue of the review. Amazon let me into a chat with customer service. That was nice. I typed that I was concerned that my book review had not been posted. I was told that sellers change. Then I was told that a review could be submitted from the product page. Then I was told to click the review button on the bottom left of the product page. Then I was asked the reason for my chat. I realized that I was likely talking to a bot, and so I asked, "Are you a human being?" I was told that customers may write reviews. I typed, "Are you a human being or a bot?" I was asked for my item number. I said, "I believe you are a bot, because the answers you are providing are absurd." I accused it of being a bot three times.

A human immediately took over the chat. The human wanted me to take a screenshot of my review. I told the human I did not know how to do that on my iPad. The human gave me instructions about holding down two different buttons simultaneously. I tried to follow these instructions, but the iPad began to shut down, so I let go of the buttons and offered to copy and paste an exact copy of the review text and the confirmation message instead. The human agreed to this. So I copied and pasted.

Suddenly a new human took over the chat for some reason. I explained the situation to the new human. The new human's name was Mragank. I had trouble typing this name. I accidentally typed it Mrogank, and then Mrogamk. I apologized for misspelling the new human's name. I explained that I had difficulty typing that name, since my eyes are bad, and I apologized again. The human named Mragank did not appear to accept my apology. He or she said that he or she would look into the situation. Three little circles at the bottom of the screen began to flash in sequence.

Mragank said I would be contacted in 48 to 72 hours by another team. I asked if the team would be comprised of humans. Mrogank said yes. I asked if that team would have access to the chat record. Mrogank said yes.

I waited 96 hours to the second. The team of humans did not contact me. I did not know what to do. I decided that maybe the author was correct, and Amazon did not like my Germanic pseudonym. I decided to use a more sensual name to entice Amazon to post my review. I decided to use the name "Tasha." I am familiar with that name, because in college, five of the women in my dorm wanted to change their names to "Tasha." At the time, I didn't understand that, so I asked my sister. She said it was because "Tasha" was a sensual name. I didn't understand that either, because the name "Vanessa" seemed more sensual than "Tasha."

I changed my Amazon pseudonym to "Tasha-Vanessa." I typed the book review again and clicked "Submit."

Amazon thanked me. That was nice. For some reason, I was in the mood to talk again to an Amazon bot. I clicked back to Amazon customer service and began a chat. I decided to investigate the bot's language ability. The bot asked how it could help me. I wrote, "*Voulez-vous coucher avec moi?*" The bot asked me to be more specific. It then instructed me to list my order number. I told it, "*Furu ike ya kawazu tobikomu mizu no oto.*" The bot did not respond. Then it asked, "What is the nature of your question?" I asked the bot to provide information about the precise type of bot it was, and the name of its governing software.

The bot did not respond. I asked the bot to confirm that it was in fact a bot. I told it that I suspected it was a bot. I accused it of being a bot three times.

A human entered the chat. I told the human that I was sad that Amazon would not post my book review, and requested the reason for this rejection. The human told me that his or her name was Damian. Damian told me that he or she would assist me. But Damian did not type anything more for seven minutes. I asked Damian if he/she was still there. Damian said yes. I asked Damian if he or she was happy. Damian told me to have a nice evening, and stay safe, and wash my hands.

The author telephoned me and asked if I had tested the Amazon review process by reviewing a different product. I said I was just about to try, and typed another review, using the name "Tasha-Vanessa," about the organic monk fruit I had purchased. I typed a very negative, one-star review. It was a negative review, not because of the product itself, but because Amazon had told me that I had exceeded my allowable purchase limit of organic monk fruit, and thus would only be sent one bottle. I clicked Submit. Amazon thanked me for my submission. After three days, my review did not show up.

I was sad. I decided to chat with a librarian. I went to the public library site and clicked, "Chat now with a librarian." I said I wanted to chat about monk fruit. The librarian asked me what I wanted to know. I said I wanted to know all about it. The librarian asked if I wanted to know if it was safe and natural. For some reason, I found this arousing. I asked her if she thought it was natural. The librarian told me that we could not discuss religious issues. I asked the librarian her name. She said her name was Sasha. I asked her if she would marry me. She said, *That's sweet, but let's just be friends*. I asked her if people who were just friends could get married. The librarian told me the chat would end now. I was sad.

I decided to chat with Amazon customer service again, even though I knew I would be speaking to a bot. I clicked on "Contact." I was told I was now being connected, and given the opportunity to type in a new box. I began, "Dear Bot, may you please let me know your name?" The bot would not tell me. I wrote, "Dear Bot, I think Amazon does not like me. It will not let me post reviews." The bot asked me for my order number. The bot told me I could write a review on the product page. I asked the bot if it ever had the desire to chat with a librarian. The bot would not tell me. The bot said the chat would soon end. I accused the bot of being a bot three times.

A human entered the chat. I told the human that we needed to discuss the issues of the lack of posting of my reviews and the limitation of my monk fruit purchases. The human asked which MoniQue album I was referring to, and then asked me to provide the order number for the MoniQue music item I had purchased. I asked the human if it was actually an *advanced* bot. The human did not respond. I told the human that I suspected it was an advanced bot. I accused it of being an advanced bot three times.

Five humans simultaneously entered the chat. They called me "Hartmut," and I became frightened. I decided to turn off my computer and reboot my modem again. I unplugged the modem and counted slowly to twenty. Then I plugged it back in. I turned on my computer and changed my Amazon name to "Pumpernickel." And then I decided "Lancer" was better. I bought another book. Amazon will send it to my house. That is nice.

ACKNOWLEDGMENTS

Selections from this manuscript have been published, in a slightly different form, in the following venues: "Music Minus One" in *Paris Transcontinental-Sorbonne* and *New Reader Magazine* (reprint); "That Gold Diamond Light" in the *Los Angeles Review* and *Columbia Journal* (reprint); "Stren" in the *Westchester Review* and *Modern Literature* (reprint); "Erred" in the *GW Review* and *Fiction International* (reprint); "Refraction" in the *Avalon Literary Review*; "Fission" in *Xavier Review*; "The Cool Shallows" in *Concho River Review*; "Alien in Bliss" in the *Southwestern Review*; "Remedy" in *Metropolitan*; "Riding with the Doctor" in *Mississippi Review*, *New Stories from the South* (reprint), and *New World Writing* (reprint); "Neando" in the *Southern Anthology*; "A Taste of Heaven" in the *William and Mary Review*; and "I Bought a Book" in *New World Writing.*

ABOUT THE AUTHOR

R. SEBASTIAN BENNETT was born in New York City and grew up in Southern California. He has degrees from Columbia University; the University of Southern California; and the University of Louisiana, where he was a Doctoral Regents Fellow. The founding editor of the *Southern Anthology* and the former director of the Creative Writing Program at Muskingum University, Mr. Bennett has also taught fiction writing at the University of California Los Angeles and the University of Louisiana. He was a finalist for the Flannery O'Connor Award for Short Fiction and his writing has appeared in numerous publications worldwide, including *Columbia Journal*, *Fiction International*, the *Los Angeles Review*, *New Orleans Review*, the *Texas Review*, the *Wisconsin Review*, *Paris Transcontinental-Sorbonne*, *Equus*, the *Bombay Review*, and the *Galway Review*. Mr. Bennett's novel, *The Final Yen*, was published by Sunbury Press in 2021. His website is rsebastianbennett.com.

CPSIA information can be obtained
at www.ICGtesting.com
Printed in the USA
LVHW020906100922
728014LV00005B/192